May all the dragons you meet

Seymour

THE LAUGHING PRINCESS

THE LAUGHING PRINCESS

by Seymour Hamilton

illustrations by Shirley MacKenzie

Published in Canada by Colophon

2016

Library and Archives Canada Cataloguing in Publication

Hamilton, Seymour

The Laughing Princess

ISBN 978-0-9949499-3-6

Published by Seymour Hamilton

This is a work of fiction. Names, characters and incidents are the products of the author's imagination. Any resemblance to actual events, or persons, living or dead, is entirely coincidental.

Cover and internal illustrations by Shirley MacKenzie www.artspace59.com
Edited by Jessica Knauss Acedrex.com

Publication History
First published by Açedrex Publishing, 2012
Published by Açedrex Publishing, 2013 (New cover by Shirley MacKenzie)
Published by Açedrex Publishing, 2013 as *La princesa valiente* (Translated by Susana Martín Puya)
Published by Açedrex Publishing, 2014 (Cover and illustrations by Shirley MacKenzie)
This illustrated edition republished in Canada by Seymour Hamilton, 2016

CONTENTS

one

THE LITTLEST DRAGON

There came the time in which we now live, when princesses are rarely seen outside picture books, wizards are met only in stories, and dragons eke out a mythical and heraldic existence on shields, flags, badges — and perhaps in the minds of those who yearn for a simpler age.

Into this rational but anxious time were born two children, a sister and a brother. They were well fed, well loved, well dressed and well educated, and they knew that if only their world lasted another lifetime, they would surely acquire a generous share of its goods and pleasures. Their names were Petra and Daniel, and they were both of that special age at which they had discovered that their parents did not always understand them.

They had been taken by trains, airplanes, cars and ships to a little remote Village at the foot of great mountains that rose out of a fjord as deep as the peaks were high. They were on holiday, but since neither Petra nor Daniel had been consulted about their destination, they were not overjoyed

1

when they arrived on a rainy day when the clouds clung to the knees of the mountains, the sea mist rose up the cliffs, the pines dripped onto the rocks below and the stone houses of the Village huddled damply together within the constant sound of the surging sea.

The next day was no better. While their mother and father exclaimed about unspoiled beauty, traditional architecture and unchanged folkways, Daniel and Petra were bored by the rain-soaked Village that smelled of fish, and wished for the entertainments to which they were used in their city home. The voices of the Villagers were slow and slurred in their ears, the children of their own age who they saw from time to time in the Village square had no attention to spare for tourists, and did not even give the visitors' bright holiday clothes a second glance. The inn at which they stayed was filled with adults who frowned if Petra and Daniel so much as ran down the stairs, and it was too wet to play outside.

When they awoke on the second day and saw raindrops sliding down the windowpanes, Petra looked at Daniel and Daniel looked at Petra and without a word exchanged between them, they decided to sulk. They tagged along behind their parents, had their photographs taken in front of the ruined Castle, their tummies filled with cakes and pastries between meals that left them groaning from overindulgence, and their feet were made sore from walking on cobblestone streets while their parents conducted an implacable search for anything old enough to be picturesque and odd enough to be called quaint.

They stared at coats of arms in a museum and saw a bewildering assortment of dragons rendered in ironwork, paint, wood, glass, picture books, and even on needlepoint chair backs and quilts. Daniel broke their sulking pact to stick out his tongue in imitation of one of the more horrendous dragons — a sea monster holding a girl in its claw — and Petra laughed before she remembered that she was trying to maintain a day-long frown.

The third day was as bright as the preceding two had been grey and misty. The rain pools dwindled among the cobblestones, the sun warmed the pines so that they perfumed the air, and old men came out of nowhere to sit on bollards and benches at the edge of the quay which formed one side of the Village square. Their seamed and wrinkled old faces impassive, they sucked on pipes and stared out of rheumy eyes at the fishing boats, no doubt thinking how much easier it was for today's sailors than it had been when they were young.

After breakfast, Petra and Daniel were informed that they were to amuse themselves — a prospect which appealed only slightly less than spending the day feeling seasick on the small and fishy boat which their parents had hired to take them up to the head of the fjord. Feeling abandoned, banished and rejected, the children sulked and pouted until their faces were sore from keeping air in their cheeks and frowns on their foreheads.

A friendly waitress in a blue gingham dress presented them with boxes containing lunch, and told them of a little beach beyond the Castle where she had played as a child. They said a polite and insincere thank you, and set off across the square, splashing their feet in the few remaining puddles.

Petra and Daniel followed a grassy path along the cliff-top to the seaward side of the ruined Castle. Beside the massive granite walls was a flight of broken stone steps that ran from a battlemented tower, down over the cliffs to where waves splashed into bright spray against a rocky breakwater. Protected by encircling cliffs and the remains of a stone dock was a little bay edged by a sun-warmed beach. The children soon forgot their ill humor as the magic of the meeting between land and sea claimed them, and they climbed carefully down the ancient steps, eager to explore.

Before long, Petra had a pile of shells that had been curiously shaped and polished by sand and sea water, and also a damp smudge across her forehead to which her fair hair clung. Daniel's left foot was wet from slipping on a seaweed-covered rock, his curly red hair was filled with sand from trying to see into what might have been a cave in the cliffs, and his pockets clinked and bulged with the smooth stones he had collected.

When they sat down to eat their lunches on a piece of granite bigger than a dining room table, it was only with difficulty that they remembered to complain.

"Nothing to do," said Petra, nibbling on a hard-boiled egg.

"Not one solitary thing," agreed Daniel around a mouthful of smoked herring.

"Awful," said Petra.

"Dismal," said Daniel.

They finished their shortbread in silence broken only by the sounds of the sea and the creaking cry of gulls that circled overhead, looking for scraps. Daniel threw his apple into the air and they watched the birds squabble over it until one particularly large and fierce gull flew with his prize up to the top of the Castle's crumbling battlements.

"Bet you I can skip a stone seven times," said Daniel.

"Bet you can't," said Petra.

Daniel managed five on his first try, six on his second, and then Petra lost interest after a succession of threes and fours.

"Seven!" he yelled, and turned to see his sister bent over the shells she had gathered, her hair curtaining her face.

"You never," she said.

"I did. It was a beauty. I bet there isn't another skipping stone like it on this beach. In the whole world, maybe."

"Bet there is. You can't find it, that's all," said Petra, and went on arranging her shells into interesting patterns.

Daniel started to search for another well shaped stone. He walked along the edge of the sea where the ripples left salt foam on the sand, and he stepped onto clinking shale that had fallen from the cliffs into the shadows below. Near the cave-like cleft in the rocks that had fascinated him earlier, but into which for some reason he had not wanted to venture, he stumbled and looked down. There was a stone round as a coin, polished as a jewel, smooth as a china saucer. It fitted his hand comfortably, and when he moved into the sun and stroked it with a curious finger, it warmed to his touch.

"I found it!" he shouted. "Watch me!"

Petra glanced up in time to see Daniel's arm swing back. She looked out at the water to where the splashes would come, but nothing disturbed the ripples on the little bay.

"Ha!" she said derisively. "You dropped it."

When she looked back at her brother, she saw that he was holding his hands in front of him and staring at them intently. Wondering whether he might have hurt himself, she left her shells and walked to where he stood.

"It spoke to me," murmured Daniel, and then looked at Petra. "How did you do that?"

"What?" asked Petra.

"Make your voice go all hissy and squeaky," said Daniel. "'Don't you dare,' you said."

"I did not," she replied.

Daniel shrugged and raised his arm again to throw the stone.

"Throw me in that cold water, and you'll be sorry," said a small voice.

Daniel looked at Petra, and Petra looked at Daniel, and they both stared at the stone in Daniel's hand. The rounded rock swayed back and forth on his palm, then split open. With the sound of a peculiarly strong eggshell breaking, two thin husks of stone fell onto the beach, and in Daniel's hand was a tiny winged creature.

"It's a bug!" said Petra.

"I am not a bug," said the small voice. "Insects don't have scales."

"It's a snake," said Daniel.

"I am not a snake," said the voice clearly. "Snakes don't have wings."

"Then what are you?" asked Daniel.

"I'm a Dragon."

They stared at the little creature, which flexed its emerald green wings, swung its pointed ruby-red tail and opened its mouth to display needle-sharp fangs no bigger than those of a mouse.

"It's beautiful," said Petra.

The Dragon nodded.

"I know," it said proudly.

"I'm going to throw it into the sea," said Daniel, who was confused, nervous and felt the need for decisive action.

"Do that and all your hair will drop out," said the Dragon. "You'll be an old man just as quickly as I can say the words, and you won't like it a bit."

"Go on," said Daniel. "You're too small to hurt me."

"All right," said the Dragon. "I'll give you one more chance. Look up at the top of the Castle wall."

Daniel and Petra looked up to where the granite blocks of the fortress were a ragged line against the sky. A piece of the battlements twice the size of a chest of drawers turned bright red, flew up into the air and fell hissing into the water of the little bay where they stood.

"See?" said the Dragon. "Any more rude remarks about size, and the next time I'll choose a piece of that mountain over there, and you'll be underneath."

"Ah — would you mind if I sat down?" asked Daniel, and his knees did it for him before he could get an answer. The little Dragon was unaccountably heavier in his hand.

"Are you related to the dragons whose pictures we saw in the museum?" asked Petra.

"I certainly am," said the Dragon.

"I'm Petra and this is Daniel," said Petra.

"I know," said the Dragon. "He's the one who put out his tongue at the picture of Ke-Au-Ka Ida and the Princess."

"I'm sorry," said Daniel.

"There was a time when you'd have been turned to stone or transformed into a flounder, or at least given a plague of warts," said the Dragon. "But it's more difficult to do the magic these days. Steel ships plow the sea and it's not safe to fly above the treetops. Only the old people give us a thought — as if we were legends and dreams."

"Would you like a piece of my sandwich?" asked Petra. "There's still some left."

"It's nice to see that there still is *one* fair maiden," said the Dragon gallantly. "Thank you, I'd like that."

Petra offered a piece of ham sandwich, and the Dragon took it between two shining claws. Sharp teeth flashed, chewed appreciatively, and the Dragon grew longer by the width of Daniel's thumb.

"May I put you down on this rock?" asked Daniel.

"You don't happen to have another name, such as George or Beowulf, by any chance?" asked the Dragon.

"No," said Daniel.

"And you don't have a sword somewhere?"

"No," said Daniel.

"Good," said the Dragon. "I knew it all along, of course, but I was just checking. These days you can't be too careful."

Daniel gently lowered his hand and the Dragon walked with dignity to the top of the sunlit rock. It coiled its tail on the stone and stretched its wings with the rustling sound of fine steel being sharpened.

"Right," said the Dragon. "Make yourselves comfortable, because I'm going to educate you."

Petra and Daniel looked at each other.

"Oh no," said the Dragon. "Not your sort of education. None of that foolishness of proving theories or testing hypotheses or learning to juggle imaginary numbers. I'm going to tell you a story."

"Oh good," said Petra. "I like stories."

"All right," said Daniel. "But we won't have to answer questions afterwards, will we?"

"Of course not," said the Dragon. "Any worthwhile story is complete when it's been told and heard. All you should do is tell it again. Now listen carefully."

And as Petra and Daniel leaned forward, the Dragon told them the tale of a princess and a sea dragon.

two

THE LAUGHING PRINCESS

She was a sailor, she was a princess, she was beautiful and she loved life. That is not to say that she was always happy, but only that when she laughed, she did not hold back, and when she cried it was never for show.

She woke early, dressed quickly, took her sailor's knife and ran down the stone steps that led from the Castle to the quay where lay her boat, the *Spindrift*. The little vessel spoke to her of freedom as surely as when she had astonished everyone by choosing it as her birthday gift. Her father had expected her to ask for costly jewels and dresses, but though such things also gave her pleasure, they were not to be compared with the love of wind and water she had discovered as a child.

She loosed the braided ropes that held the trim craft bobbing in the protection of a rocky breakwater, hoisted the sail, and steered beyond the headland out into the open sea. At first, the *Spindrift* rose and fell to the confusion of waves that pounded the steep shores, but soon it danced to the rhythm of the seas rolling out of the endless ocean to the west. She smiled as the spray flew on each side of the dipping bow, and she shook her fair hair free to be tugged by the wind that pressed against her body. Lips parted in delight, she cheated speed out of the air and water and felt her land-bound worries drop away into the white wake behind her. When the shore dwindled until the trees were a dark green blur and the breakers at the base of the cliffs had become a thin line, a flash amid the cresting waves caught her eye, and she steered towards it.

Before the *Spindrift* reached the spot, she laughed again, this time in greeting to the dolphins which broke the surface and rolled on their sides so that their wise eyes could see the little boat and its lone sailor. They swam on either side of the *Spindrift*, playing their game that brings delight to every mariner's heart, pacing the boat and diving across its bow to prove their skill and speed superior to any wooden vessel made by the hands of men.

Slipping a leather thong around the tiller, the Princess tied the mainsheet around her waist. She threw her head back, took a deep breath and plunged into the sea to let herself be towed behind her boat amid the dolphins. Twisting and curving her body as they did, she was at one moment in their cold green element, and the next catching a quick breath as she, too, sprang exultant into the air. Their smooth, hard bodies slid against hers, and her hands touched their slick skin. They played together, and between woman and dolphins was a bond of wordless delight.

Six times the Princess plunged below the surface, six times they accompanied her, their perpetually smiling faces close to hers. The seventh time she directed herself deeper, accepting their challenge to dare the dark water. But as she strove to imitate their skill, the rope from the

Spindrift slackened, and she lost the precise timing with which she had moved so surely. Instead of rising in a glorious rush to the shimmering water's surface above her, she was tugged lower and still lower. Her boat had slowed and no longer pulled her back to her own world. Exhilaration turned to pain, the pain became torture, the torture an insidious demand that she slacken her will and let the sea rush into her lungs in what would be her last breath. Clenching her teeth so that they bit into her soft lips, she plucked at the knot by her waist. Her fingers fumbled with the sea-wet rope until she remembered the little knife she wore around her neck, and cut the cord with its bright blade. The Princess kicked the coiling rope away and thrust upwards. She swam with all her strength in the dark water crushing down upon her, but the surface was too far away.

Even as she knew herself to be lost, the certainty of death did not extinguish her bright spirit, and in the clarity at the very edge of life she had no regret. As her lips parted to return the dolphins' smile, she was suddenly caught in a mighty grasp. Faster than the dolphins swam, she was lifted to where sea and air met, and through the surface of the water to her native element once more. Her spent breath released in a huge sob, she drew fresh life in one ragged gasp after the other.

When at length she was able to look about her, the Princess became aware that she lay across the palm of a vast hand, shadowed by arching fingers overhead, warmed by the life that pulsed beneath her. She looked outwards to the horizon on every side, and saw only the waves' heave and roll. She looked down between the sinewy fingers, and saw the green-scaled breast of the immense sea creature that had rescued her. Again she laughed, this time simply because she was alive.

Lit from within by sea-green fire and charged with the wisdom of immeasurable age, a great eye looked down upon her from under a forehead that eclipsed the sun, and the Princess knew the Dragon Ke-Au-Ka Ida, and was known by her.

"Mortal child," said a voice so gentle that the Princess's laughter turned to sudden tears. "Why is it that you should have dared my element so boldly?"

And the Princess said the first words which rose to her mind, and as she spoke, she felt them to be true.

"I came to test myself and venture out beyond the land. I wished to share the innocence of dolphins who know nothing of the statecraft for which I am valued by my father, the dynasty to which my mother would have me bear sons, the ambitions of the men who would be my lovers."

"And why, my child, do you flee those who lay these claims upon you?"

"Because they want me only for what I may bring to them, and not for what I am. In me they see riches, power and pleasure. They do not know or care for my desires."

"And what do you want, my child?"

"To give, and not be used; to love, and not be owned; to become, and not to be molded by another's will."

There was a silence filled only by the ceaseless sounds of the sea, and the Princess thought deeply of the times when she had put aside her selfhood and craved approval from those around her.

The eye of the Dragon Ke-Au-Ka Ida glowed with a tender light.

"My world knows no statecraft, and my lovers have no dynasties to maintain," said the elemental. "My children I bear because they make me what I am, and my joy is that I bring forth their lives to do with as they wish. I grieve at their sorrows, and I weep if they are taken by death. But I do not cease to be, and dare, and risk the ever-moving present, whatever it should bring."

The Princess stood upon the Dragon's hand and made obeisance to Ke-Au-Ka Ida. She bent one knee, and stretching out her hands, bowed her head in reverence.

"Great mother, I am answered," she said. "I, too, will seek to be, and dare, and risk."

Ke-Au-Ka Ida closed her huge eye, and a deep knowing flowed between elemental and mortal. The Princess shared in the Dragon mother's power, and understood how she would always be whole, no matter how she gave her mind, her body or her love.

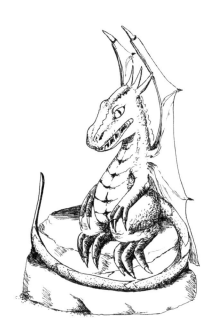

The Dragon's laughter was as waves flung high in storm and tempest, and the Princess laughed as well. Ke-Au-Ka Ida raced to the horizon and captured the little fleeing boat, still chased by dolphins. The Princess stepped from the elemental's hand into the *Spindrift*, and turned her slim vessel towards the land where lay her destiny.

When the Dragon finished his story, Petra and Daniel both held their breath for a few moments, and then they both sighed at the same time.

"That's the breakwater, and this is the little bay where the Princess kept her boat," said Daniel.

"And she ran down the same steps we did," said Petra.

The Dragon nodded and its eyes blinked slowly. The pointed tail swung back and forth a couple of times, and then curled around the top of the rock.

"She was special," said Petra. "I'd like to know what happened next."

"I want to know more about Dragons," said Daniel. "Are they all huge and fierce on the outside and all soft and gentle inside, like Ke-Au-Ka Ida? — I mean, except for you, of course," he added, when the Dragon's slit pupils focused on him.

"Dragons come in a variety of shapes and sizes," said the Dragon. "We don't all look the same, or behave in the same way. We're individualists."

"I thought Dragons were supposed to breathe fire," said Petra. "But Ke-Au-Ka Ida lived in the sea."

"Then I shall tell you a story about a fire Dragon."

And the Dragon began the story of The Wizard and the Fire Dragon.

three

The Wizard and the Fire Dragon

Peder the Charcoal Burner, known to some as Peder the Wizard, stamped around his cottage, pulling at his beard and muttering to himself.

"Fools," he said, as he poked the fire under his kettle. "It's one thing that the price of charcoal doesn't make it worth my while to cut wood and stack it, but it's quite another matter when people haven't got the sense they were born with. Here's the whole Village with sore teeth and rotting gums, catching cold at the first puff of a wind, and yet they won't eat the plants that keep me fit."

He stroked his whiskers flat against his chest and glowered into his teapot. The day before, he had pushed his way through hip-deep snow all the way to the Village, a pack load of supplies from his root house on his back, but to no avail. A night's sleep had only brought him greater anxiety for the Villagers, coupled with exasperation at their refusal to see reason.

"I even tried to give my herbs away," he went on, spilling boiling water onto the dusty floor as he made rose hip tea. "But they muttered about witchcraft and necromancy and sorcery, and dropped them in the mud. What do *they* know about sorcery?"

He puffed at his tea, sipped it and scalded his tongue, which did nothing to improve his humor.

It had been a winter in which the herring had chosen not to come to the coast, and also one in which a succession of villainous storms had. Hardly a boat dared cross the harbor bar for weeks on end, and the people were reduced to living on leathery salt fish and starveling coneys that had ventured out of the forests for lack of their own food. The storms had swirled snow into great drifts down to the water's edge and the sight of the mountain peaks was a memory.

"For twenty years I studied to become a wizard," said Peder while he waited for his tea to cool. "Then I gave it up to cut charcoal and learn about living things instead of spells and runes and pointless cabalistic lore that never once worked — unless it was to make me the butt of jokes and ridicule."

He swallowed a long draught of tea and grimaced. While he had been talking to himself, it had become cold. So he tossed the lees into his fireplace, hung his mug from a hook on the mantletree, took his cloak from the peg behind his door, and walked out of his cottage into steadily falling snow. More to relieve his feelings than out of any thought of being useful, he took his axe and started to split wet wood into wetter kindling. As he worked, the snow eased and wintery sunshine lanced among the branches in shafts of light made visible by the curling flakes still eddying among the pines. He took off his cloak, trudged back to his cottage where icicles dripped from the eaves, and hung it on a gnarled stake. The shoulder-tall shaft of oak had once been his wizard's staff, but he had decided that it was more useful for drying his laundry.

"Twenty years," he said thoughtfully as he looked around the little valley where he lived. "Twenty years when I could have travelled the world, or raised a family or made a fortune — perhaps all three. And I had to spend it all looking for wisdom. Perhaps it's I who's the fool."

He went back to splitting and stacking wood throughout the rest of the day, pausing only for his lunch of an apple and some cheese, the one wooly and wizened, the other runny and rancid. When evening came, he thumped his axe into the chopping block and frowned at what he had accomplished. Without planning it, he had cut, split and stacked a substantial charcoal rick ready for firing.

"Now why did I do that?" he grunted. "I must be losing what little sense I ever had. Perhaps it's the result of all those tongue-twisting incantations that never raised anything but dust — and the occasional belch from all the meals I skipped."

The thought reminded him that it was time for his supper, so he walked back to his cottage in the fading light of a pinkish sunset and used the end of the cheese to savor a vegetable hot pot made with wild onions and bullrush roots.

When the moon rose and a silvered beam slanted through his window to dull the candle he had lit, he wrapped his cloak around him and took his mug of tea out to a large flat stone near his doorstep. He kicked the snow from its black surface, and sat down cross-legged with a sigh. The moonlight was bright enough for him to trace the symbols he had once inscribed into the slab of rock. It had come from an outcrop near the head of his valley, and had been his altar in the days when he labored to master the mystic powers in which he no longer believed. Now he remembered only his long struggle to skid the stone across the snows of a winter almost as late as this one was proving to be.

He sipped at his tea, enjoying the taste of rare oils and roots he had infused into the dark brew. The moon swung overhead and its cold light etched black shadows around the charcoal rick. Peder spilled the dregs of his tea onto the stone and idly drew his finger back and forth, feeling the runes he had carved so many years before.

Without warning, the valley was plunged into darkness. Peder looked up, expecting to see clouds covering the moon, but instead a piece of the night sky fell towards him, darker than the spaces between the stars. A rushing sound was in his ears, but not a hair of his head was disturbed.

With a leathery clap like a hundred whips snapped at the same moment, and a sudden gust of furnace-hot wind, the charcoal rick burst into flame. Orange tongues of fire licked up at the sky, and yellow light flickered in Peder's eyes, making him blink. He rubbed his hand across his face, and when he looked again, in front of him was a creature so overwhelmingly, unthinkably, unbelievably terrifying that his mind refused to accept what he saw.

"Hallucination," he said, and rubbed his eyes again.

When he opened them, a sea of flame was around him, lapping the stone where he sat, curling back at its edges in fiery crests. He felt his whiskers crisp and heard the hair on his head crackle, but the fire was held back by an invisible wall.

The flames rose and met in a blazing arch above him, then fell away. Instead of melted snow and the ruins of his cottage, Peder saw that his valley was unscathed. The charcoal rick blazed, challenging the light of the moon, and amid the pyre was a Dragon. It was five times the height of Peder's cottage, and it burned with the fierce glow of a long heated poker. Its body was black, its talons etched in scarlet, and its long neck a ropey column wreathed in smoke.

Twisting fumes enveloped the head that bent towards Peder, and the voice he heard was made of exploding sparks and crackling embers.

"Speak," hissed the Dragon.

Peder was speechless.

"Lost your voice, wizard?"

Peder shook his head.

"Then ask."

"Ask what?" asked Peder, with a cough.

"The usual supplication is for power," said the Dragon like pine branches thrown on a bonfire. "But you may have wealth, or fame, or long life, or knowledge, or the endless service of all you enslave to your will."

Peder pushed back the edges of his scorched mustache with one thumb, and tapped his teeth thoughtfully with his finger nails in a habit he had acquired over his years of puzzling over cabalistic lore. The eyes of the Dragon flickered, and the fire was drawn around it so that flames licked its gold-veined sides and glinted on shimmering scales.

"I think I'd like people to know me for what I am," said Peder.

The rippling flames around the Dragon's head puffed out, and white moonlight gleamed on the coruscating surface of its awesome head. It stretched its long neck upward as if to bite the moon from the sky. Peder shuddered.

"Impossible," said the Dragon. "You ask never to be misunderstood, and even I, Ena-Pingala Kythe, am not comprehended by my fellow elementals, let alone the groveling men who have summoned me with their sacrifices."

"I'm not groveling," said Peder. "And I didn't make any sacrifice to you. My search for power ended years ago."

The Dragon hunched into glowing coils and extended its long neck so that its head was above Peder's rock. Hot breath swirled downwards, and the stone cracked along its length, splitting down the line of runes carved upon its face.

"Neither you do," mused the Dragon, its eyes molten diamond. "Thus I will give you a spark of my eternal fire. You will burn with the knowledge of your own selfhood and your joy will be to feel the vital spark in each living thing. You will be gladdened by the existence of every man, woman or child you meet, even as I rejoice in the infinite variety of their lives."

The Dragon leapt upward into the night, and the last vestiges of the charcoal rick scattered in pinwheeling shards. The altar stone crumbled into sand. Peder stood up a little shakily.

"I don't feel any different," he muttered. "Perhaps I should have asked him how to get the Villagers to eat more sensibly."

As Peder slapped dust and ashes from his cloak a voice hissed down out of the night.

"Brew them some fermented spruce beer to gladden their lives and revive their bodies."

The moon winked into darkness, and a comet trail spangled the sky. Peder stroked his fire-shortened beard thoughtfully.

"Good idea," he said. "I wish I'd thought of that."

"He wasn't much of a wizard," said Daniel. "I'd have asked for something more than *that*."

"Would you?" asked the Dragon, re-coiling its tail half-way down the rock and rustling its wings.

"I think he was nice," said Petra. "Sort of like our grandfather, only lonelier."

"I'd have laid one of my spells on Ena-Pingala Kythe, so I could have him back when I wanted him. It would be really neat to have your own Dragon."

"You have much to learn about Dragons," said the Dragon. "We are not owned — and we are dangerous."

"You mean, like the rock you threw into the bay?" asked Daniel.

"A trifle," said the Dragon. "I was in a good mood. Now, if I'd just woken up and was feeling out of sorts... then you'd find out why mortals say, 'Let sleeping Dragons lie.'"

"I thought that was about dogs," said Petra.

The Dragon snorted down its nose, and the air grew perceptibly warmer.

"How soon they forget!" it said. "Very well, you shall hear about a blind man who woke a Dragon, and of the exchange they made."

And the Dragon told the story of the Elemental Exchange.

four

ELEMENTAL EXCHANGE

Talking to a Dragon is of all conversations the most dangerous. It is not that Dragons are evil. It is that Dragons know your hopes and fears. They are elementals, beyond mortal concepts of good and ill. Their minds are filled with the experience of millennia, and to them pleasure and suffering, joy and sorrow are as the shapes of clouds at sunset.

The Dragon Aina-Lani Kahu-Wellan raised his head from the mountain pool, and let a draught of water roll down his throat to mingle with the subterranean streams that flowed within his mountainous body. He unsheathed a claw that girt one of the ranges that were his hide and idly scratched an avalanche off his southern massif. A Village that had sprung up in his last few centuries' sleep disappeared under the rubble of a collapsing foothill, but he paid it no heed. Even the ache of loneliness for the time when he had sported in the fire of a younger world had long since joined pity and forbearance in some lost crevasse of memory.

He shrugged a scaly wing and forest hillsides crumbled. His yellow eyes blinked slowly, and he reached out in his imagining to search for what had roused him. Now that he had drunk his fill of the emerald lake around which he lay in a cordillera of stony folds, he was calm, but deep below, his sulfurous fires churned with the lava of implacable life, and he sought a reason for being and doing. Would he rise up on his mighty wings and roast a glacier into a sudden torrent? Or stretch out a claw and make new canyons and defiles amid his rocky domain? Perhaps he might lay waste the plains in one blast of drought and destruction, renewing himself in actions the world had not seen for generations of mankind.

He blinked again, and directed one hooded eye down to the tiny figure which had troubled his mind even when he slept. Below the precipice of his chin, beneath the seracs and hoodoos which were his teeth, down, down to the lakeside where his chin had rested, he cast his gaze. At the outlet of the lake, trebled in size now that his head no longer blocked the water's way, a man clung to a boulder, half in the sudden spate of frothing spray, half spread-eagled upon the ragged rock. As the Dragon watched, the first flush of water dwindled to a trickle, and the man staggered to his feet, one hand groping for the staff that dangled from a leathern thong around his wrist.

Aina-Lani Kahu-Wellan cleared his throat of the gravel from centuries' disuse, and spoke.

"Man, I am curious why and how you have disturbed my rest. Your kind have scaled my flanks and stood upon my crags and troubled me no more than the eagles whose generations have flown above me while I slept."

And the man raised his head to the bellow of sound that thundered around the lake, and whispered.

"I did not come to wake you, but to find my own awakening from the illusions in which I have dreamed I lived."

And Aina-Lani Kahu-Wellan heard the man's speech in the terrible power of his ancient mind, and the great Dragon's puzzlement grew, for there was no fear in that small voice.

"And now you know that I am the mountains you have seen at sunset when my backbone is the ridge that cuts off the last red rays, are you awake?"

The man nodded, but that was enough.

"Good," said the Dragon, and his word split rock. "Now you may reach into your small soul to find the most precious thing in your life, and bargain with me to spare you."

And the man knew what and who he meant, and at the same moment, that he was himself known.

"A woman," mused the Dragon. "A mere woman whose life is no less ephemeral than your own. What is that to me? Can you not imagine gold and rubies, imperishable diamond, or even the rage of a mortal who knows he must die? Can you offer me no more than this weak memory of passing pleasure? What have I to find in your soft tenderness on which I can brood while I sleep away another space of time that to you is an eternity, and to me is as a summer's evening?"

"I do not offer anything to you, Dragon. You cannot have my memory, nor the woman who is its origin. You may rend me to bloody gobbets or smear me across the valley with one of your mighty claws, but I will not surrender the treasure of my memory to you."

"What?" asked the Dragon. "You will not bargain for your life with this one miserable possession?"

"No," said the man.

"Then feel your mind taken into my timelessness and experience the emptiness that I know, who am forever alone in the magnificence of my eternal solitude. Raise your head that I may suck out your joy."

And the man's head was raised, and the yellow eye of the Dragon pierced downwards more keenly than any eagle searching for its prey. Aina-Lani Kahu-Wellan's avaricious intelligence bent its primordial energy to scoop up the memory it did not want, but needed to possess simply because it was gainsaid him.

The Dragon's eye sought the windows of the man's soul to enter at his pupils and scour him clean of his essence and his past. The elemental's mind reached out through his hooded yellow eye, but was defeated. Below that awful head, a faint sound echoed among the splintered rock, and the Dragon knew that what he heard was laughter.

Then range on range of his huge bulk stirred, and a continent shuddered to his earthquakes.

"Pitiful mortal, do you dare to mock me?"

"You mock yourself thrice over, Dragon," replied the man. "Once, that you desire what you cannot feel, twice that even by my death you will be thwarted, thrice because I am blind and all your magic is powerless to enter my mind's eye."

The Dragon slowly blinked as he directed the full force of his thought upon the frail mortal. Deep below memories piled over the eons when he had woken to ravage the world, to rise and challenge the light of the sun in his burning fury, to fly above the rocky wreckage of twisted ranges, jagged horn-bergs and glaciered sierras, Aina-Lani Kahu-Wellan recalled the terrible secret that gave him power, and he was shamed because he could not feel as did the mortal whose life he was about to end. And in that moment, he was himself transparent in his thought to the man he intended to devour.

"You are eternal, elemental, timeless, all-destroying," said the man. "But you do not and never shall know the treasure in my mind that my woman has set there. Thus, I pity you."

Lightning smote down the precipices, rocks flew from the heights, and devastation was where the Dragon's talons churned the bedrock, but the man stood firm and laughed once more, because he knew that Aina-Lani Kahu-Wellan had trembled. Preparing himself as best he might for his death, the blind man braced himself on his staff for whatever might follow. The avalanches rumbled into silence and the tremors subsided. The earth no longer shook as the great being lowered his chin so that once more his head became the crags and peaks to which the man had climbed.

"Man," said Aina-Lani Kahu-Wellan. "Live out your tiny life. Whether or not your memory stays green, whether or not your love returns your devotion, whether or not you stumble and fall on your blind journey back to her, you have braved my wrath unflinching, and I honor you by my amazement. Your treasure is in your own keeping. I cannot take it, though while I outsleep your brief life, I shall ponder the name of the power by which you guard the memory of your woman."

"Then freely I give you the answer," said the man. "The power has one simple name, and that is *love*."

He turned, and heedless of the baleful yellow eye that watched him tap his stick upon the rocks, took his way back down the mountain in search of the woman he loved.

⁂

"That's beautiful," said Petra, as the Dragon finished his story. "He loved her so much that even Aina-Lani Kahu-Wellan let him go."

"I suppose if you sleep for thousands of years, you have to have something to dream about," said Daniel. "But it sounds pretty boring. Don't Dragons have fun, like people?"

The Dragon's tail stirred the sand around the rock on which he crouched, and he raised an eyebrow. Daniel frowned, because the eye that watched him was now at a level with his head, and was at least as big as his own.

"It seems to me," said the Dragon, "that people are the ones who often lack the ability to, as you call it, 'have fun.' I remember a time..."

The Dragon paused and Daniel fidgeted, wondering whether he had offended.

"Oh, do tell us!" said Petra.

The Dragon shrugged its wings, cleared its throat, and began the story of The Solemn Son and the Boulder Roller.

five

The Solemn Son and the Boulder Roller

There was a woman who had seven sons. Six of them left her home where the pines hung their dark branches over swift mountain streams. One by one, they took the shadowy, winding path down to the Village at the head of the fjord. The seventh did not follow in any of their footsteps to become sailor, trader, soldier, blacksmith, shipwright and yes — a thief of hearts musician.

The Seventh Son was as solemn as his nearest brother was full of mirth and jollity. He helped his mother, uncomplainingly chopping wood for her ovens that yielded the bread and cakes that the whole Village agreed were beyond the envy of the most shrewish housewife in the little community. He seldom smiled, and when he did, it was so awkwardly that people looked at him as if a fish had whistled or an eagle pecked corn. The Villagers ignored him, and he never earned a second look from the young women whose covert glances assessed every male for later discussion in giggling coveys after the day's work was done.

"There's no life in that one," said the prettiest girl in the Village, and nobody would contradict her.

The mother of the seven sons, who knew all there was to know of the laughter and tears, the scrapes and adventures, the delights and distresses of raising children, sometimes despaired that her youngest was fated to live a life forever shadowed by his serious turn of mind. She encouraged him to find fulfillment in a skill, but he fumbled knots, miscounted money, cut himself on swords and daggers, hit his thumbs with hammers and barked his shins on saws. The one time he touched his brother's harp, he contrived to break two strings and scratch its smooth curves. When her first six sons agreed as one man that they would not have their youngest brother for an apprentice, their mother was too astute to argue. She learned to accept his wooden-faced presence in her life and to thank him for his earnest desire to please, but it was often that she shook her head as she watched him go about the painstaking chores with which he filled his days.

One morning as she dusted flour onto her hands and prepared to knead the dough that soon would be baked to golden loaves of bread, she looked up and saw her Solemn Son walking towards her through the clearing where stood their cottage. Overhead a lark soared into the sky and rained down his song on the whispering pines, the scarlet spires of the flowers that the Villagers called Gnomes' Pokers, and the tossing heads of ripening grain. Amid all the splendor that made his mother's heart quicken with the delight of living, his face was no less wooden than the fuel he brought for her ovens.

"Son," she said as gently as she could. "Spend this wonderful day doing as you please for a change. Wander the high paths and breathe the clean air of the mountain meadows. Take a girl by the hand and run with her through the flowers. Whistle tunes to the echoes and listen to them return your song. Go and have fun."

The Solemn Son stacked his load neatly on the woodpile and looked at his mother with eyes that had seen nothing of the beauty around him.

"Why?" he asked.

"Oh, for goodness' sake," she snapped. "Because I say so, if for no other reason. Take your dismal self out of my sight, and don't come back until you can tell me you've been happy."

She immediately regretted her exasperation when she saw him turn away, but she could not suppress her wish that whether it was grief or gaiety, something would shake her son out of his unnatural tranquility. So she slapped and pummeled at her dough, and ignored the stoop-shouldered figure that plodded up the path and into the forest.

The Solemn Son walked mechanically, neither paying heed to the subtle smells of the pines nor to the rushing of the stream in the valley below. He searched for a purpose in following his mother's orders, found none, and thus continued to put one foot in front of the other, methodically seeking he knew not what, why or how.

Eventually the path doubled back on itself and crossed a stream on a broad tree trunk cunningly felled to take the traveler dry-shod above the rushing water. His boot heels sounded hollowly on the wood as he walked from under the trees into the sunshine. A sudden glitter of light reflected from the swift water as it rushed over the stones, cascaded down crevasses and roiled and coiled in eddying pools. Bewildered by the sun-spangled, sound-drenched splendor, he halted in the middle of the narrow bridge and shook his head to clear it of a new sensation he did not recognize as wonder.

And as he stood irresolute, there was a knocking of boulders, a rattling of stones and a grinding of pebbles. The stream erupted into spray, rainbows arched and fell in kaleidoscoping color around him, and he was drenched by water cold as the glaciers from which it had come. A fusillade of gravel struck at his boots and stung his shins, and a great rock shattered the bridge into splinters and bark. He fell feet first into a pool of water so cold that he was numbed in two heartbeats. The swift current twirled him around and around and emptied him down a spillway of moss-slick stone to plunge into another pool, and then another. At last his flailing arms and legs wrapped themselves around a fallen tree, and he held himself against the current. Then he gasped and struggled his way into the shallows to stand shin-deep and disconsolate. Somehow he had lost a boot, and a pink streak of blood from one bare toe discolored the clear stream.

He knuckled water from his eyes and pushed his wet hair back from his forehead just in time to see a boulder bigger than his mother's bread ovens rumbling towards him. He tried to run, but the stream clutched at his ankles. The boulder bounced high and smashed down in the middle of a pool, drenching him once more. For the first time in his life the Solemn Son muttered a curse.

"Oh poop," he said.

It was a pathetically innocuous remark, but it relieved feelings he had never felt before.

"I'm wet," he said unnecessarily. "And I'm also angry," he added.

He glared at the boulder, and then remembering what he had seen his brothers do when angry, he kicked it as hard as he could. A howl of anguish proclaimed that he had chosen the bare foot for his revenge, but he had the satisfaction of seeing the boulder move. Then as it rocked back and forth in the stream bed, the Solemn Son's eyes widened in amazement. The rounded stone split open and unrolled itself into a scaly creature. Balanced on short, thick legs and a long crusty tail was a body many times the size of a man, crowned by a head so massive and rock-like that it was as if a piece of a mountain had taken life. The Solemn Son looked up into two eyes flecked with gold and lit by irrepressible good humor.

"Why don't you watch where you're rolling?" he demanded, careless of consequences.

The Dragon raised the fringe of roots that his eyebrows most resembled, and ran a tongue over its tombstone teeth. It chuckled with the sound of a gravel avalanche. The Dragon twitched its mighty arms in what might have been a shrug. The huge mouth gaped in a grin so wide that the Solemn Son had one glimpse of a cavernous throat before he was blown flat on his back in the water by the force of the Dragon's thunderclap laugh.

"That's enough!" shouted the Solemn Son as he got back to his feet again. "I've been drenched, pounded, rolled, bruised, bumped, soaked and toe-tortured, and I won't have any more of it."

43

The Dragon threw back its head and once more bellowed with laughter. It thumped its scaly sides until they rattled like firebricks in a jolting cart. It smote one of its upraised knees a tremendous slap, waved its tail high above its back — and overbalanced into the pool from which it had climbed. The Dragon thrashed its tail and twisted itself upright, the gold flecks in its eyes gleaming and the leathery tongue lolling to one side as it splashed to its stumpy legs. The Solemn Son's face flexed unused muscles, and his teeth flashed white in a grin of satisfaction. He heard a hesitant laugh he was surprised to identify as his own. The rocky cleft where the stream ran threw back an echo chorus. Back and forth bounced his laughter, and then suddenly the sound redoubled a hundredfold as the Dragon joined in. Man and monster sat in the shallows, shouting with glee.

At length they chortled and chuckled themselves to a silence in which they hugged their sides to ease the marvelous pain. The Dragon stretched out a hand capable of plucking whole trees as a man might pull a woodland flower. The no-longer-Solemn Son took the smallest finger in a parody of a handshake that struck both of them as hilarious. The huge hand beckoned, and the boy stepped confidently forward to be taken into a great embrace. The Dragon coiled into its boulder-rolling shape, and launched itself into the stream, protected by its scaly armor. Together they rumbled down the stream bed, flew over the edge of waterfalls and splashed into the pools below, all the way to where the stream rushed past the house where the seven sons had been born.

The mother of seven sons was stacking loaves of bread to cool when she thought she heard laughter. She listened, and heard it again, but closer. She looked out her cottage door, past the bread ovens trickling white smoke into the evening air, across the meadow to the edge of the

44

forest. Her seventh son limped towards her through the flowers, occasionally bending to sniff a bloom and chuckle to himself. On his face was a smile that lit his eyes as never before.

"Mother!" called the ragged figure as he neared the cottage. "You'll never believe what I've been doing."

The Dragon looked at Petra and Daniel and nodded its head approvingly at their grins.

"All the way down the stream, thump, bounce, splash!" said Daniel. "That would be fun."

"It must have surprised his mother," said Petra. "Imagine living with a sourpuss like that, and having him learn to laugh in just one day."

"She burnt the bread on the first day, and on the next the loaves rose three times higher than usual," said the Dragon solemnly.

"Go on," said Daniel.

"Cross my wings and fly backwards into the sunset if I tell you a word that isn't the perfect truth," said the Dragon.

"What about her other sons?" asked Petra. "I bet there's a story about the Thief of Hearts."

The Dragon looked down at her thoughtfully.

"You want to know about falling in love?" he asked.

Petra nodded and Daniel turned his head away as if fascinated by a seagull hovering over the bay, but the Dragon knew he was still listening. Folding his wings so that they hung over his scaly back down to the beach, he began the story of The Thief of Hearts and the Dragonets.

46

six

The Thief of Hearts and the Dragonets

The name of the thief of hearts musician was, appropriately enough, Felix. He was not only a happy man, he also had the knack of making others happy. When he picked up his harp, none could resist a certain softening of their lips and a subtle tensing of their cheeks, and before long they were smiling, tapping their toes and beating time.

There was no question that Felix had powers. His deedle-um-deedle music made people dance, his why-oh-why music made them cry and his long arpeggios and glittering glissandos made men adventurous. And it was not only the men: Felix discovered at a young age that if he so much as glanced at a girl while he played, something warmed within her that made her eyes wide and her breath come short. Then he found that if he chose to serenade one special person who caught his eye, she was drawn to him as surely as if he had taken her by the hand.

It was a dangerous life to be a thief of hearts, for he never knew when a girl might not already have a suitor or husband capable of breaking his harp into kindling and himself into stew meat.

However, despite a few narrow escapes involving back windows, bare feet, moonlight and brief leavetakings, neither Felix nor his harp had ever suffered more than a few scratches. Moreover, no woman had ever complained.

Felix led a happy life, giving and taking pleasure in his talents, remaining unscathed by the woes and sorrows that were visited on less fortunate folk. However, there came a day, then a week, then a month, then what seemed to him forever when he ascended beyond happiness to rapture, then fell to depths of despair he had never imagined. Nonetheless, to his surprise, he survived. In between these pendulum swings of mood and emotion, he swung like an airborne hawk, not knowing whether to stoop earthward or be carried aloft on the winds of chance.

It was in one of these moments that Felix wandered into the forest, his harp as always over his shoulder. He left the sharp smells of the sea and the buffeting of winds driven across the endless ocean to wrestle with the mountain peaks, and he plunged into the green and silent world where millennia of fallen pine needles made his steps soundless. The scent of growing things wrought a calming effect upon his mind, and as he walked, something that would not go into words plucked at the hem of his thoughts. He took his harp from his shoulder, knelt beside a shard of stone and began to play in time to the beating of his heart.

It was no known tune that coiled into the forest air, neither was it a composite of the many airs, songs and dances that he knew, nor was it indeed a product of his will. Rather, music flowed from him and he felt himself somehow apart, both watching and hearing what he was doing as if another played. He forgot his lover, his joys and his sorrows, and at the same time knew that the melody was made of all three.

When he was finished, his breath and blood seemed drained from him. He sank back against the mossy rock, closed his eyes and hung outside of time for a little while that to him was an eternity.

He woke from his reverie to a rustling by his ear. It was a delicate sound, like the flutter of a moth's wing, yet bright and sharp as the sound porcelain might make if it were capable of fast, flexible motion. The sound at his ear was duplicated a tone lower beside his knee, and again a minor third higher above his head. Felix lay with his eyes shut, savoring this magical music until he felt four sets of claws clutch his knee and something like the last hand span of a whip coil around his shin. He opened his eyes and looked into the gaze of a small Dragon. The creature was the delicate blue of an aquamarine jewel, softening almost to white in the shaft of sunlight where it crouched. Wings delicate as the petals of a pale rose gently fanned the air in an undulating motion graceful as the swirl of water in a fast flowing mountain stream. The Dragon's head was poised on a long neck that quested back and forth, now regarding Felix with one gold-shot jewel of an eye, now with the other. Its mouth was curled in the smile a cat might wear if it were shaped like a snake and endowed with a wisdom as old and individual as the North Star — and as bright.

"We are Twyleth Aldrenfen," said the Dragon.

"Felix the Harper at your service," said Felix.

"We know," chorused three voices in harmony. One was at his knee, one by his ear, one above his head.

Felix shifted his gaze and saw two more Dragons, somewhat smaller than the first, but no less miraculously exquisite.

"You gave us pleasure," said the small voice at Felix's ear, and the other two nodded their heads on their delicate necks in a gesture that was both proud and condescending.

"You give me... astonishment," said Felix.

"It is customary for us to offer you a wish," said the Dragon on his knee.

Felix's thoughts became suddenly both clear and apprehensive.

"Oh Twyleth Aldrenfen," he said, choosing his words with care. "May I — and this is not to be considered my wish, but only a mere question — discuss with you the nature of my desire before I ask for it?"

The wings of the Dragon on his knee rippled, and Felix was sure that he had just seen a miniature, ironic shrug.

"Intelligent mortal," said the Dragon at his ear, with a hiss that might have been laughter.

"Perspicacious, prudent, and most pre-sumptuous," said the Dragon above his head.

"We grant your request," said all three, in voices that melded together in counterpointed harmony.

"I love a woman who is as none other..." began Felix.

"Piffle," said the Dragon above his head, who was now perched on the rock against which Felix leaned. "You've said that a hundred times or more."

Felix tried to continue. "Her lips are as..."

"That, too," said the Dragon at his ear, and for emphasis drew its scaly tail across his neck.

"If she pledged her love to me, I would forsake all others and be true to her alone," said Felix.

"Doubtful," sneered the Dragon on his knee.

Felix took a deep breath and let it all out again. His fingers flexed around the neck of his harp.

"I love her as I love my music, and I can only live if both are in this world," he said.

The Dragons exchanged glances first from one eye and then from the other.

"We would live together in a cottage by the sea, and..."

"Grow indifferent to each other as you realized that you were no longer in love," completed the smallest Dragon.

There was a silence broken only by the rustle of delicate wings.

"I can imagine no other woman who I would wish to bear my child," said Felix softly.

The Dragons moved their heads in unison, and Felix looked where their long necks pointed. There in the air above him he saw a figure he recognized as himself, and beside the apparition was his love.

"My Princess!" gasped Felix.

As he watched, the vision blurred, and both figures grew older before his eyes. He frowned as he saw bright blonde hair dull to grey, and his own face become wrinkled. Time touched the two again, and they were stooped and twisted by the years, their clothes in rags. They looked at each other, and their faces were blank. Finally, the woman stood alone, and then she, too, was gone.

Felix clutched his harp and drew it close to him, for in none of the visions had his image held an instrument. The strings hummed as his fingers touched them, and the curve of the wood was warmed by his body. A horror possessed him as he thought of a future in which was neither music nor the love he had so recently found. The Dragon on his knee stared at him fixedly, its gold-veined eyes blinking slowly and its mouth curled in a sardonic grin.

Anger rose in Felix. He drew his fingers across the strings of his harp, and the forest rang to a melody that was near to a lament yet that also spoke of iron determination. As he played, he spoke to the Dragons, his music weaving a spell to which the creatures swayed back and forth.

"Oh Dragons," said Felix. "Nothing I say is proof against your wisdom or the chances of time. You tempt me to despair with your images of what might be, but you also provoke me to the knowledge that there is but one thing I can ask of you."

The Dragons' heads rose and fell as six golden eyes scrutinized the mortal. Felix's harp was plucked from his grasp and held in mid-air beyond his reach. He sprang to his feet, the Dragons whirling around his head in a blur of shimmering colors as they flashed from sunlight into shadow.

"Give me my harp!" he demanded.

"Is that your wish?" whispered the whirling Dragons.

"Yes!" shouted Felix.

He caught his harp as it fell. For a long moment he stood aghast at what he had said. Then his fingers fell into their accustomed places and he swept the strings in ringing chords.

"I was going to say," he said to the empty forest, "that I wish for no contrived future, no magic power to bind, no single wish that we might later regret. I was only going to ask that..."

A triad of voices spoke out of nowhere.

"That you and your love should follow your nature and destiny," said the Dragons. "And you have your wish."

The harp in his hands received a feather-light touch, and when he looked at its head, the smooth wood was ornamented with three tiny Dragons, no bigger than his finger's end.

"And did he marry his princess?" asked Petra, her eyes shining. "I liked him. He didn't want to trick her. He wasn't *really* a thief at all."

"I want to hear about the son who was a soldier," said Daniel. "I bet he had a sword and lots of adventures. I'd rather own a sword and go to all sorts of places than have an old harp — even if it did have a Dragon on it."

"You'd like attacks and ambuscades, night forays and desperate odds?" asked the Dragon.

Daniel nodded. He stood up and waved an imaginary sword.

"I'd be quicker than a flash of lightning, and stronger than a... than a...."

He was going to say, "Than a Dragon," but when he looked up and saw the underside of the Dragon's chin, he decided that it would be better to sit down quietly.

"Tell us about a soldier," said Daniel politely. "That is, if you'd like to."

And the Dragon told the story of The Warrior and the Trickster Dragon.

56

seven

The Warrior and the
Trickster Dragon

Barrin was a strong and sudden man. He was magnificently muscled, copiously scarred, and he carried a huge sword across his back. Barrin was a warrior, and proud of his trade.

He had come to the sleepy Village as bodyguard to a wealthy merchant who had a beautiful wife he cherished only a little less than his gold. Barrin had led a pack train through mountains that held whirling storms, dreaded avalanches and bandits no less fierce than the land where they lived. Five times had the brigands fallen whooping upon the pack train to pillage its booty, and at every assault Barrin's sword had whistled its deadly song. He had smiled grimly when the ponies shied away from headless figures huddled in the snow as they picked their way around earth dark with the blood of the attackers. Each evening the merchant's wife had admired him as he sharpened and re-sharpened his great sword. He accepted her adulation, barely noticing her fragile beauty, and though the merchant's fussing and fuming affected him not at all, Barrin made no response to her fluttering eyes and parted lips.

A pouch of gold at his belt, a memory of the merchant's wince at his handshake, and the satisfaction of counting the bodies he had felled were enough for Barrin as he sat within a tavern, his long sword across his knees. The fishermen gave him elbow room and more as he drank the best the innkeeper could offer. There were no songs that night, for those who piped up a shanty, hummed a love-lilt or sang the first words of some drinking song were soon hushed. Men glanced out of the corners of their eyes at Barrin and watched him with sidelong glances as hesitant as those of the fearful boy who kept his tankard full.

When he had drunk his fill, Barrin slapped coins on the table with such force that they dented the battered wood. One leg of his chair snapped as he stood and hitched his sword over his shoulder, and the door complained on its hinges as he thrust it open. He adjusted his bright armor and his eyes flickered up and down the darkened streets in search of possible foes. He shrugged, kicked the door closed behind him and strode towards the sea. When he reached the headland, he stopped below a pinnacle of rock where the grasses were stunted by the sea winds, slapped his breastplate and let his cloak fall to the ground.

Barrin cracked his knuckles, set his teeth, and began the nightly martial exercises he did no matter where or what the weather. High above the sea that sucked and heaved below the cliff top, the moon shone pale light upon a lone figure and his intricate, deadly dance. The great sword leapt forth and cut a whispering tune in the sea air, Barrin's armor clinked and clashed, and his feet now touched the short grass light as a girl, now thudded firm to give him purchase for the thousand and one strokes of his whirling blade. First with one hand, then the other, then with both he strained his knotted muscles till they gleamed in the moonlight and sweat stood out on his brow. Again and again he sheathed his sword only to snatch it forth in the glittering arc of destruction that had been the last sight of so many.

At last, he slid the keen blade into its scabbard, tightened his belt, and leaving his right arm bare to the night wind, he settled his cloak clear of his weapons. One thumb tucked into his belt, fingers caressing his dagger, the other hand curved to curl around his sword's hilt, he glared at the moonlit sea.

Over the night sounds of sea and wind came a mocking laugh. In an instant, Barrin was tensed for the shock of combat, his sword sliding from its leather scabbard. Poised in a fighter's crouch he swung to attack whoever had crept up behind his back. His dark eyes flashed in the silvery light as he turned his head to one side and the other, but he saw nothing but windswept grasses and broken stone.

"Come at me, then," grunted Barrin. "Do your worst before you die."

A light laugh was in his ears, close enough to touch. He leapt and turned in the air, his sword sweeping out towards the cliff top, but again nothing stayed the blade's murderous sweep.

"Show yourself!" shouted Barrin.

He faced the path he had followed to the lonely place, and saw a horned shape, broader than a bull, taller than a man, scaled in purple armor. Without a moment's hesitation, Barrin's sword cut at the monster. He struck with his full weight behind the blow, his wrists ready for the moment when steel cut through flesh and bone. Instead, he was whirled about by the sheer force of his own attack as his sword met only air. Recovering in an instant, he turned full circle, parrying the cut he felt sure would be aimed at his back. He crouched and brought his sword upward to sheer away the hand he knew was poised to strike, but again his sword met nothing.

The monster was gone, but in its place a woman was stretched languidly in front of him. Barrin's fury glinted in his eyes, and he struck downward. As the sword descended, he saw wings no mortal ever owned. His blade slammed into the grass and rang on a stone a hand span below the earth. Jerking it free, he advanced once more to where a coiled serpent blocked his way. This time he thrust before him in the lunge that had spitted many an unfortunate attacker, but as he saw his blade pass through the serpent's head, he heard a ripple of delighted mirth. Again his wrists were cheated of the tendon-straining death blow.

"Brave fighter, have you nothing more that you can do?"

The amusement in the voice drove Barrin into frenzy. Stamping and slashing, he hewed at the air until his breath came short. As he recovered from each fruitless blow, he saw another form at which to cut. Serpent became soldier, soldier turned to archer, archer to unicorn, unicorn to woman, woman to fish, fish to bird, bird to priest, priest to naked man, man to child, child to infant — and Barrin struck at them all.

The baby smiled up at him as his sword drove through its chest and deep into the ground. The body vanished, and Barrin tugged at his sword, unable to withdraw it from the earth. He strained at the hilts, his shoulders creaking and grinding.

"Barrin, Barrin, what kind of a man are you?"

He leaned on the sword and clenched his fist on his dagger, but the voice was everywhere.

"A warrior," he growled between clenched teeth. "I live for battle. I test myself in combat. I am alive when I am threatened and I fight. I am completed when I strike home. All else is waiting and preparing for the next time."

"And have you found foemen worthy of your zeal?" the voice taunted.

"Show yourself, and feel!" shouted Barrin. "I have felled soldiers, brigands, thieves, and I have never turned from battle until the last blow was struck."

"True, oh mighty Barrin," said the voice. "And how many have you killed?"

"This week, fifteen," said Barrin.

Up the path came fifteen shades of men and boys. The moonlight shone through them and they cast no shadow, but their features were clear and their eyes looked into Barrin's as they filed past him.

"See, Barrin, who you killed. Two grandfathers, six boys, seven starving men."

"They came by night, or out of the sun," grumbled Barrin. "They had weapons, they attacked, I slew them."

"These, too?" asked the voice.

A double column of ghostly shapes walked soundlessly towards him. Their ranks separated around him, and the shades trod onward over the cliff top and out into the air. Up the path came more and more: men, women and children who turned their faces towards Barrin as they passed, and expressionlessly walked on.

"I did not kill them," said Barrin. "The mark of my sword is not on them."

"These are the wives, the children, the families of those you killed. You were the death of them as surely as of those whose lives you took with your swift sword. They are your victims, for they died because of you."

"I didn't start it!" yelled Barrin. "I'm a warrior, not a king or councilor who plots and plans wars. I go where I am needed, do what has to be done, kill clean."

"Was this a clean kill?" demanded the voice, as a woman passed him bearing her dead child. "Or this?" it asked, as a little barefoot boy limped by.

"I was beset, surrounded," muttered Barrin. "They were all around me in the darkness, and I struck out lest I be killed."

"They were children, Barrin."

"Enemies," Barrin tried to say, but the word froze on his lips.

He yanked at his sword, and it came free as if nothing had held it. The ghosts of those he had killed winked into nothingness, and instead he faced the Dragon Gregilshen-la Gladgly in her true form. A talon reached out, and Barrin glanced down to see a sign scratched deep on his breastplate.

A wordless cry of blind fury came from his distorted mouth, and he hacked at the Dragon with all his strength. This time he felt a shock numb his palms as his sword clanged against his foe. Again and again as he swung his sword, the blade rang and shuddered in his grip. The Dragon's head was above him, its neck extended, and he hewed at its purple scales in one last paroxysm of fury.

When the Villagers found him the next day, his notched sword was in his hand. All else had been driven beneath the earth by the great stone that had fallen upon him.

Daniel shifted on the stone where he sat, and said nothing.

"Do you still want to be a warrior?" asked the Dragon.

Daniel concentrated on the pebbles between his shoes and did not look up.

"He was dreadful," said Petra. "I'm glad he's dead. Killing all those children! That's awful. Only a man would do that. Gregilshen-la Gladgly did the right thing. I just wish...."

"What do you wish, Petra?" asked the Dragon, looking down at her with a gleam in his eyes.

"Oh!" said Petra. "Not a *wish* wish. Just a wondering kind of a wish."

"Wishes can be dangerous, Petra," said the Dragon. "More dangerous even than warriors."

And the Dragon told the story of Ryll's Fortune.

eight

Ryll's Fortune

Ryll was the daughter of the luckiest man in the Village. From her mother she had inherited good looks, and from her father good humor and an ability to get what she wanted.

"Tell me what you did today," he would say to her when she came home from play with pine gum on her hands, leaves in her hair and rents in her clothes that made her mother shake her head and purse her lips with annoyance. But her father would not have her punished. "Clothes are cheap and life too short to be bound by a needle and thread," he would say.

And Ryll would speak of what she knew would please him. She told him that her dolls were prettier than those of other girls, that she had won at games even when she had not, that she was envied by other children of the Village whether or not they did, and she never failed to tell him if a servant, a sailor or any other of the many men and women who worked for her father had failed to be polite and pleasant to her. At this her father's face would darken, and Ryll would smile secretly to herself, knowing that the person she had named would be punished.

One day, when Ryll was a woman in every respect, her mother took her aside to talk about the future. This was not the first occasion when Ryll had been subjected to advice, but this time her mother's seriousness was not to be deflected. They sat together upon costly chairs by the fireside, and Ryll looked at the fresh stacked wood ready for the evening, trying to appear patient. Around them were the treasures her father had imported at great price: paintings bought from penniless monasteries, furniture made of dark exotic woods and rich colored fabrics from the south, and glass ornaments so delicate and fine that there was no way to tell that they had come from the fierce heat of ovens over which men wasted their youth and health.

"You must decide among Evan, Brian and Carl," said her mother. "And you must do it today."

"Why?" asked Ryll.

"They have been waiting on you now for more than six months, and you should tell them which one is to be your choice."

"What is it to me if they choose to waste their time?" asked Ryll.

Her mother's eyes narrowed, and her face no longer recalled the beauty that she had passed on to her daughter. Ryll examined the lines notched between her mother's eyes and resolved not to frown lest she, too, lose her good looks.

"It's one thing to be fetching," said her mother through pursed lips. "But quite another to be complaisant. Now consider. Evan's father is the second wealthiest man in the Village. And he's good-looking too, with that black hair of his. Mark you, Brian's mother is of the Castle. With your good looks and the dowry your father will provide, there could well be preferment for both of you, particularly since they say that Brian has the King's eye. Indeed, he is a handsome lad, much as your father was at his age."

"And Carl?" asked Ryll, though she knew the answer.

"A dreamer, a wastrel, forever off nobody knows where. Even when he's talking to you, it's impossible to tell what he's thinking. Don't tell me you favor *him*?"

Ryll shook her head so vigorously that her red curls swung across her face. Her mother could not see whether her vehemence was negation or refusal to speak, which was as Ryll wished, because there was more that could be added. Carl was the son of a poor fisherman who lived on the north side of the Village in a cottage which could have fitted into the room where they sat.

Nevertheless, she felt something for Carl which was different from speculations about the property and place the other two could bring her. Carl offered only himself, and he was by far the most handsome of the three. What was more, he wrote her poems, brought her little carvings of animals that he had made himself, and never failed in a politeness that contrasted with the self-confident rivalry of the other two young men. However, she offered Carl nothing but scorn if anyone else saw him near her, and she never missed an opportunity to mock his threadbare clothes, down-at-heel boots and the shoddy jacket he wore against wind and weather whenever he stood in vigil beneath her window — which was often enough to be quite pleasantly flattering.

"Well, I'm glad of that," said her mother as Ryll settled her hair with one smooth hand. "Your father would like you to encourage Evan," she went on, settling herself for a lengthy conversation in which she would be the only speaker.

"I'm not ready, and I haven't decided," said Ryll, examining one pink fingernail. "As father says, 'There are always more fish in the sea.'"

"There may be more fish, but that doesn't mean you can catch them," said her mother. "And speaking of fish, it has been two years that the catch has been good, but you never know what might happen. Your father is a generous man, but he can only give you of what he has."

Ryll's eyes narrowed, and a thin line furrowed her brow. She had not thought of this before. What if her father were to die? She imagined herself at his funeral, dressed in black with a hint of white lace at her neck, and two big tears welled up in her eyes, for practice. She would turn sorrowfully away from the young men, and they would become tender and manageable in their care for her grief.

"We discussed it last night," said her mother. "And he said 'I'm not as young as I was. Ryll should be married, and soon.'"

"I don't believe it," said Ryll, her eyes wide with anxiety. Could it be that her father had a premonition of his death?

"My dear, would I lie to you?" said her mother. "Those were his very words. And since you are his dutiful daughter, you should heed them."

Ryll stood up and looked around the room. She thought how good it would feel to own all that the house held. She would sleep with her husband in the big room upstairs, and he would make her father's fleet of ships bring them still more money every year. Perhaps she would redecorate the house in more stylish colors. Maybe she would be able to travel with her husband and choose beautiful things that would even be the envy of the Castle. There would be parties — after a proper period of mourning, of course, and best of all, her mother would not be able to tell her who to talk to, what to eat or when to go to bed.

"My mother lives with us, but she is stricken with sorrow now my father is dead," said Ryll soundlessly to an imagined room full of people.

How everyone would admire her for her graciousness as she stood at the center of her party wearing imported silks and satins, while her mother in widow's black sat quietly in a corner. They would all know that Ryll was now the mistress of the house, and compliment her on the improvements she had made. There would be dancing and laughter, and everyone would say what a good hostess she was. She would be invited with her husband to the Castle and they would outshine the Prince and Princess.

"Ryll, I really shouldn't tell you, but your father is thinking of buying you that little brown house only two streets away and giving it to you as a wedding present," said her mother.

Ryll stiffened, and her greenish eyes flickered as she glared down at her mother.

"I must think," said Ryll. "Alone," she added, when her mother's mouth opened to speak.

Seething with disappointment, Ryll stamped her feet as she walked towards the big front door. Then, remembering that Carl might well be waiting outside, she turned and left the house by another door, snapping a rebuke at one of the maids who was in her way. She chose the alleyways and back streets that led away from the Village square, not wishing to see anyone she knew until she had resolved how to achieve her desires.

When she came to the stream that separated the fishermen's cottages from where the wealthier people lived, she splashed across the ford, soaking the hem of her dress. Once in the northern part of the Village, she walked more slowly, conscious of the fact that she was now among the homes of the rough sailors who manned the ships her father owned. A ragged pair of children looked up at her from some game involving an old bait bucket and a pile of stones, and Ryll crossed the lane so that she would not have to look at their grubby faces. She enjoyed a brief moment of pleasure in the fact that her everyday dress was of a better quality than the little girl might ever hope to wear. Then she thought of having to leave her father's beautiful house, and her face darkened into a frown. She hurried on, ignoring the people she met.

When she was beyond the last house, Ryll took a path that led towards the mountains. Wrapped in her covetous thoughts, she climbed upwards, oblivious to where she was going.

When a bend in the path enabled her to see over the tops of the trees on the slopes below, she looked back at the cottages and shuddered. *How dreadful it must be to be poor*, she thought, and resolved not to accept anything but the best of what the world could offer. Then, because she could not decide how to arrange her future to coincide with her desires, and did not want to return until she had a plan, she continued to climb the path to the mountains.

At length, she paused by a stream, wishing she had thought to bring some of the new rolls she had smelled as she left the house. The rushing sound of water calmed her mind somewhat, and she looked up into a sky blue with the rich warmth of summer and scattered with rising puffs of white cloud. An eagle spiraled high above her, its pinions steady as it unerringly rode the air currents as surely as a horseman on a beaten path. As Ryll watched, she saw the bird pivot neatly around in a circle, and then change the slow rhythms of its gliding into a strangely purposive flight unlike the effortless scanning with which it patrolled its vast aerial kingdom. She squinted against the bright light, and then rubbed her thumb across her brow quickly when she remembered the lines on her mother's face. She shaded her eyes, and saw four more eagles in straight and level flight towards a pass between two of the northern mountains at whose feet lay the sea.

"Perhaps it's an omen," she said. "People who are as important as I am sometimes receive guidance. Yes, that's what it must be."

Making the best speed she could, Ryll struck out from the path through the thinning trees towards the shattered rock fallen from the peaks that flanked the pass. Soon she was among stunted bushes, and it was not very much later that she climbed over grey shards of tumbled stone. Her expensive shoes hurt her feet, but she was overwhelmed by the conviction that something important awaited her. Heedless of danger, she toiled upwards as if possessed. Occasionally her step loosened a boulder to fall rattling below her, sending echoes bouncing from the sides of the mountains, but her urgency was too strong for her to feel afraid of the heights to which she had climbed.

When her dress caught on a rocky outcrop, she paused beside a sentinel stone to look upward once more. The blood beat in her ears and she could feel a pulse throb at her forehead as she narrowed her eyes to scan the bright sky. She stretched out a hand to steady herself against the cold rock, and felt disappointment keen as the wind that poured down from the heights to pluck at her clothes, because she could no longer see the birds she had decided were her guides. Ryll began to worry about getting back to the Village, but as she was about to start down the mountain, out of the corner of her eye she saw something move against the sky. Soaring upward on the wind, the five eagles appeared from behind the pass, circled once in tight formation, then flew off in different directions as if drawing an invisible star in the sky.

"Come back!" shouted Ryll. "Tell me where to go!"

She stamped her foot in anger when the birds paid her no heed. Tossing her wind-tangled hair back from her face with a jerk of her head, she clenched her teeth.

"I won't give up!" she said. "I'll have what is mine."

Her stubbornness set her thinking, and she reasoned that the cause of the eagles' strange flight had to be beyond the crest of the steep slope only a short climb further. Once more she struggled upwards over the jumbled stone until she reached the summit of the pass. Ryll shivered as the wind whipped her skirts around her. She looked down into a hanging valley green with larches and jeweled by a string of vivid blue pools. At first, there was nothing on which she could fix her attention that could possibly account for the eagles' flight. Then she saw a fine column of smoke rising into the air.

Without stopping to wonder why the mountain winds had not torn apart the thin white wisp, she started down the other side of the pass at the run. Her feet found a way that took her safely amid the debris of winter avalanches and led her down to where moss grew to the edge of the mountain pools. Again, her dress was splashed to the knees as she waded across a cold stream and ran on numbed feet towards the beckoning smoke. She weaved in and out among the larches, their fine needles sweeping across her face and body, and she might have lost her way amid the trees that obscured her goal had she not chanced across a narrow path.

Little more than a dimple among the trees and bushes, the path hid among rocks, trees, pools and streams, but nonetheless drew her onward. It seemed made by someone who wanted no visitors, which convinced Ryll that she was nearing her goal. Her curiosity growing with every step, Ryll pushed the branches of a spreading larch out of her way and looked into a clearing rimmed by rock on three sides, protected on the fourth by the woods through which she had come. A stream chuckled at her feet, pointing the way towards a shining pool at the edge of which was a cottage.

It was not an ordinary home. Indeed, had it not been for the smoke that rose from its rough, misshapen chimney, Ryll might have taken it for a mere jumble of rock fallen from the peaks above. The roof-tree ended in a tangle of roots above two deep-set, uneven windows and an open door was flanked by two tapering white stones. The walls bulged with odd-shaped boulders, and the roof was covered in moss and patches of grass.

This is the place where I will have my wishes granted, thought Ryll, and walked boldly towards the strange dwelling.

As she neared the dark doorway, someone spoke from within.

"Come and talk with me, Ryll."

Ryll stood as if rooted to the spot. Even though husked by age, the voice still held the music of youth in its cadences, yet there was also a wry humor in its tone that caused Ryll to suppress a shudder. She combed her hair back with her fingers and drew herself erect so that she looked properly important and deserving.

"Who are you?" she demanded.

"I have been waiting for you to come," said the voice from within the darkness of the open doorway.

Ryll put aside a sudden flash of apprehension, summoned her dignity and stepped between the white doorposts. At first she could see nothing. Then she recognized the shapes of a table, a chair and a bed by the flickering light of a blue-flaming fire.

"You followed my eagles."

The words were like silk drawn across a knife.

Ryll inclined her head in a slight nod, as she had done in the past to many a compliment. She peered into the gloom, and caught sight of an old face framed by white hair. The wide-spaced eyes were sunken, but they held a knowing gleam, and the lips were slightly curled at the corners, as if they had done a great deal of smiling throughout a long life.

"Have you the power to grant wishes?" asked Ryll.

"I have."

"Then don't let my hateful mother take my father's house away from me after he is dead. Tell me which of my suitors will please me most. Let my looks turn men's heads all the rest of my life. And you can start by giving me as much of the riches of the sea as can be put into two buckets like the ones I saw the children play with as I came here."

"Are those all your wants?"

Ryll's eyes narrowed as she considered what more she could ask.

"I ask only what I deserve," said Ryll.

"Then you shall have it. Take the bowl from the table and cast it in the fire."

Ryll frowned in puzzlement, but did as she was bid.

At first the blue flames only flickered more vigorously, but then the cottage was suddenly filled with smoke through which nothing could be seen.

"Witch!" shouted Ryll as her eyes smarted and her skin stung. "What are you doing? I don't believe you have any power at all. Your magic isn't working, it's only making me uncomfortable!"

An insistent whisper came from the swirling smoke.

"Call me Pu-Ahi Oheo-Wythe, for that is my real name. Are you ready to see my true shape?"

"Yes," said Ryll, and then she misgave. "No. Oh, I don't know."

"Have you come this far to go home with nothing? Where is the spirit that made you follow my eagles, climb the pass and find the path I signed for you?"

Ryll covered her face with her hands, pressing her fingers against her eyes until veils of purple, red and blue flared in her mind. She trembled, but then she thought of all she would soon own, and let her hands fall to her sides.

The cottage vanished. She stood at the edge of the mountain pool, and above her writhed a skein of smoke. As she watched, it knotted and unknotted, twisted and turned, thickened and solidified into the shimmering coils of a Dragon so many-colored and gleaming that its myriad hues wavered at the edge of whiteness. Turning about and about its undulating body, the creature's gleaming head now was obscured by leaf-thin, glass-clear, silk-soft wings, now stared at her from eyes bigger than both her hands might cover, now was hidden by a tail huge as a sail, pale as parchment, iridescent as oil on water. Out of this vast turmoil, the Dragon spoke a thousand times louder than anything Ryll had ever heard.

"Do you believe me now?" asked the Dragon.

"I do," gasped Ryll.

"Then know that I am the wind that one moment whispers at your ear of the movement in pine branches, and the next howls around the mountain peaks. I am the elemental Pu-Ahi Oheo-Wythe, and I have the power to take or make any form I wish."

The great body came lower and lower, and the dance of the Dragon's coils enveloped Ryll. She clutched wildly about her as she was raised up and up until the valley was so far below that its larch trees were as the stitches of an intricately worked counterpane. One part of Ryll's mind was panic-stricken, another quivered with anticipation for all that she had demanded. She calmed herself with thoughts of wealth, and looked down at the pass over which she had climbed.

"Look between your feet," said Pu-Ahi Oheo-Wythe.

Ryll stared down past her scuffed shoes and saw her Village rushing towards her. She was at the heart of a storm that tore into the Village square, twisted the roof off her father's house, leveled its walls and tossed its contents to the mountain peaks.

Then she was falling into blue-black clouds, unable to hear her own screams for the crash of thunder as she plummeted earthwards through stinging rain and hail. She closed her eyes tight shut lest she see the ground rushing towards her.

Then to her amazement, her feet felt the cobblestones of the Village square and in each of her hands was a heavy weight. She smiled in satisfaction, opened her eyes and looked about her. Though the sun shone and the skies were clear, her eyes were so blurred that it was some time before she saw that a new house stood where her home had once been. Out of its doors came two very old people, dressed in fine clothes and attended by servants. She would have called after them to ask about her parents, but she could only manage a hoarse whisper. And as she stood, she saw a middle-aged man walking towards her, his arm around a woman who led a child by the hand.

The man seemed familiar, but before she could comprehend what she saw, two other men walked by, deep in conversation. They paused to look at the elderly couple who had first attracted her attention.

"There he goes," said one whose face Ryll thought she recognized despite a dense black beard. "The oldest, luckiest and most prosperous man in the Village. Who knows how close we both came to his riches?"

The other laughed as they passed her, and something woke in Ryll's memory.

"Evan!" she said.

The men looked at her, and disgust was on their faces as they turned away. Ryll took a step forward, and stumbled on the hem of her dress. She looked down in dismay at the ragged, black material that draggled to the ground at her feet. She dropped what she held, and fish guts spilled onto the cobblestones from two stinking pails. She put her hands to her face in horror, and her fingertips rasped on scars and warts.

"Ugly old crone," said one man to the other. "What kind of a life must she have lived to look like that?"

"None of our business," said the other with a shrug, and they walked together towards the Village tavern.

This time, when the Dragon finished his story, it was Petra who sat very still, looking at the waves creep slowly up the beach.

"What a mean one she was!" said Daniel. "She deserved what she asked for — I mean, what she got."

"Dragon," asked Petra softly, "Do all your relatives do things to people that are so... so..." She shivered.

"Drastic?" supplied the Dragon. "No, of course not."

The Dragon sank its feet into the beach as it stood and moved so that the afternoon sea wind no longer blew Petra's hair across her eyes. Making a tent of its wings, whose topmost spurs rose three times their height, it settled down again and rested its head on the rock on which it once sat. Daniel moved closer to Petra, and they looked into the huge eyes expectantly.

"Another?" asked the Dragon.

They both nodded vigorously, and the Dragon told the story of The Poet and the Angular Dragon.

nine

The Poet and the Angular Dragon

There was a poet who had wandered from city to country to town until he owned a fine stock of memories both happy and sad. He had shipped aboard a leaky boat with a curmudgeonly skipper and had blistered his hands on ropes and fishing lines for months, until he was heartily sick of the sea. At length, he had come to the Village at the foot of the mountains that brooded in purple shadows while the clouds tore to shreds on their peaks.

After the boat had made fast to the stone quay that formed one side of the Village square, the moon rose and the snow on the crags was lit with a ghostly light. Though he had been awake for two days while his vessel was storm-lashed and nigh to overwhelmed by raging water, nonetheless the poet could not sleep. He went ashore and walked among the houses of the Village, where yellow candlelight gilded the windowpanes and silhouetted those within. He heard the murmur of voices and felt a stab of heartsick loneliness for the home to which he could never return, and a longing was upon him to stare into eyes kind enough to see him for himself and accept what they saw.

He passed a tavern, and heard the discordant sounds of revelers far gone in their cups, and he wondered why he should be restless when his fellow mariners sought oblivion in drink, or lay exhausted in salt-wet hammocks aboard their evil-smelling boat. He turned his steps southwards and walked beyond the Castle to where the cliffs drew back from a stony beach silvered by the eerie light of the moon. Shingle scraped under his heels and he drew his jacket tight around him, wishing for he knew not what.

It was not that he had lacked comrades, lovers and good friends, but they were lost along the difficult leagues he had travelled, and now he could revisit them only in memory. There had been a time when he thought to make of his voyaging a never-ending river of poems that would touch the hearts of all who heard them, but now the source of his inspiration had dwindled to a trickle of disjointed words. Whenever he took up his pen or mused over rhymes and rhythms, he was driven to the conclusion that there was no one who would care to hear what he struggled to say.

"There really isn't much point to it," he said aloud to the night.

Like all poets, he talked to himself often, but on this occasion when he tried to continue, he could manage only an ironic laugh that threatened to turn into a sob.

He kicked the stones under his feet and stared seaward at the ghost-white crests of breakers as they crashed along the shore. He shivered as he walked along the line left by the receding tide where the waves had tossed up storm-wrack mingled with ruined pieces of men's handiwork. A broken oar poked up from a tangle of twisted tree roots, and his feet crunched on the fragments of a broken bottle. Ahead of him was a wrecked boat, drifted deep into the shingle by the pounding waves. Its upturned hull was sliced into an enigmatic shape of dark, convoluted shadows. At one moment he saw a huge bird, then a coil of rope stuck with broken spars and masts, then the bony skeleton of a monstrous sea creature.

"It is a statue, created by some sculptor to tease the minds of all who see it," he muttered to himself. And then, as he knew this could not be, he asked the night, "Is nothing real? Must I choose only among illusions?"

"Can you see the wind?" asked a voice softly. "Or hear the stars?"

The poet stopped and stared about him, for in all his musings he had never been questioned so appropriately.

"Yes I can," he declared. "At least, there have been times when starlight tingled at the edge of hearing, and the wind was soft enough that I stared at where I held it in the hollow of my hand."

The poet stepped towards the figure on the boat, that now he saw was a seated woman, her arms folded about her knees.

"You bind words to escape from the knowledge that it is your own mind that shapes your life," she said.

He stepped towards her outstretched hand, then blinked and looked again. Lit by a light that was not of the moon, he saw eyes whose slit pupils watched him steadily, and he knew that he spoke to a Dragon. Such was his loneliness that he was not capable of fear. Instead, he was captivated, and saw beauty in the gentle curve of its mouth and the soft gleam of its eyes. He felt a bond between his humanity and the inhuman creature, and both his intelligence and his feelings were convinced of its gentle and kindly interest in him.

"All that opposes you is only as real as you imagine it," said the Dragon.

The poet knew that the Dragon spoke of more than the moment, and he was moved to admit his deepest sorrow and the cause of his midnight quest.

"I would know that I was heard by someone who cares whether I live or die," he said. "I wish affirmation that what I write may touch another's mind."

"Has there been no such moment for you in your life?" asked the Dragon, like a lover in whom there is no jealousy.

"Once," said the poet. "But she is far away, and I do not know whether she even thinks of me."

"Then you have touched another's life, and you have no reason for despair."

"I could be wrong," he said.

"True," replied the Dragon. "But that thought brings no hope, so set it aside."

And the poet sighed as if he had put down a heavy burden. Clouds sailed across the moon, and in the darkness he fixed his gaze on the Dragon's glowing eyes.

"Who can I thank for these good thoughts?" he asked.

A laugh like the chime of high, distant bells mingled with the sounds of the sea.

"I am she who is not as are my kinfolk, for I am further from eternal and closer to mortals than they. I speak only to poets, dancers, men and women whose lives are not complete without the tones, shapes and words that they themselves have wrought. I live by their thought as they by their arts, though I offer them only those songs, dances, forms and words that can be shared with the fewest of the few."

"But what are you called?"

"The other Dragons speak of me as The Angular One," said the Dragon, and there was sorrow in her voice. "For among my fellows I am no better understood than are you."

"Then tell me your name, oh Dragon," insisted the poet, "that I may reverence you in my poems. Because you are beautiful, and wisdom is in your words."

Again there was musical laughter to join with the night sounds of wind and wave.

"You are a persistent one, Poet," said the Dragon, and her voice was soft as a woman well pleased. "You know full well how to flatter."

"I do not deny it," said the poet. "But you can see my thoughts and know that I speak truth. My world is words, and I must have them in my head to know that I exist. Do not torture me with your silence, for I would repeat your name and know that both of us are real."

"Then I will whisper, for none has heard it for so many of your generations that I have almost forgotten how it is pronounced."

And the Dragon bent her head towards the man, and the poet heard the name Kaiwheil Bhagmani-ji, and was content. The harmony of shared compassion filled his soul, and he pressed his palms together in token of his thanks. He could find no words to thank her, so he closed his eyes to savor the syllables he had heard.

When he looked again, the beach was white with moonlight, and he faced an upturned boat. He tipped back his head and saw a shape sharp as knives and soft as a woman's lips scudding down the night wind. And the poet smiled, because he knew he would hold the moment precious, and that he would continue to search the world for the stuff of which his poems were made.

The Dragon drew its sea green wings in a little closer around the two children, and they looked out under the massive arch of leathery scales towards the little bay, now shimmering in the late afternoon sunlight. The shadow of the cliffs was almost to where the Dragon's tail lay in serpentine coils on the beach.

"I hope some day I'll be able to meet Kaiwheil Bhagmani-ji," said Daniel softly. "I'd like to tell stories and write poems."

"I thought you wanted to be a warrior," said the Dragon.

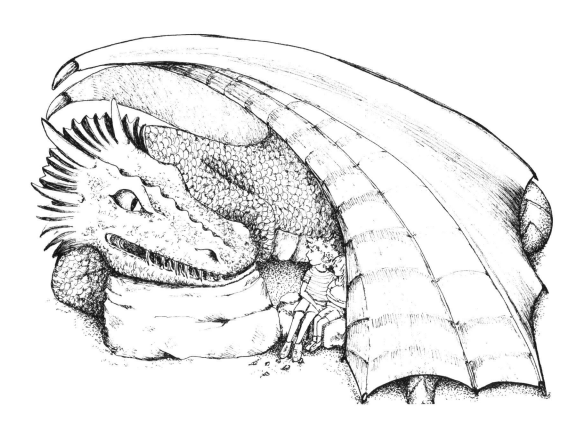

Daniel gave his head a little shake.

"Wizard, solemn son, thief," counted Petra. "And Ryll. She wasn't very nice. Do the men get all the luck?"

"I wouldn't call Barrin lucky," said Daniel. "And the Princess sounded to me as if she was going to have a good life."

"Very well," said the Dragon. "Since you have very cleverly avoided wishing for a story about a woman, Petra, I will tell you about *two* women."

And the Dragon told the story of The Witch and the Tavern Wench.

ten

The Witch and the Tavern Wench

Anna was a witch — or so thought the Villagers. They were persuaded by the evidence of her twisted body, eccentric habits and profoundly fearless way of looking through to wherever it was that any malevolent man kept what remained of his decency. For this reason she was accused of having the evil eye. Anna lived where a ragged and disused path ran towards the next settlement to the south, a distance of many uncomfortable leagues that anyone of sense knew was better accomplished by an ocean voyage — assuming there was a reason for making the visit.

Anna was dying. She was reconciled to the fact, but not to the injustice of knowing that with a little help she would be able to recover. However, for one whose spine took a bend of more than a hand span to one side, and whose right shoulder was forever hunched to her ear, there simply was no possibility of her acquiring the food and drink she needed to survive. A fever had weakened her already thin figure to powerlessness, so she lay on her bed in her cottage and attempted to leave this world with dignity, whether or not anyone else should know. She resented that both she and the cottage needed cleaning, that her lamp no longer held oil, that her books were too heavy to be held in her emaciated fingers, and that the end of her nose itched. However, since there was nothing she could do about any of these discomforts, she lay and talked to keep up her courage as she prepared for the last and most daunting step for all humankind.

"Wishing is what keeps us hoping," she whispered. "I've wished for a strong body many times, and even though I couldn't have one, the wish always came just as I found out that I knew something strong-bodied people seldom learn. I suppose it all balances out." She chuckled. "All this knowledge, and nobody to tell it to. What a waste."

She focused her brown eyes on the light that came through the open door, and saw a larch tree glowing in the light of the early evening.

"That's a blessing," she said soundlessly. "A larch like a flame of living gold. A good sight for my last evening. I don't suppose anyone could ask for more. But I do: I wish I had a daughter who I had seen grow to womanhood, whose sorrows I could have met with understanding and whose joys would have warmed my thoughts. Oh well."

She closed her tired eyes, and listened to the evening sounds. A magpie chuckled and chortled to itself, the soft wind rustled the larches and swept dead needles into drifts at her doorway. She deliberately turned her thoughts towards all the happy moments she could remember, and was in the process of recreating the details of a particularly delightful night she had spent laughing with Peder the Wizard fully twenty years before, when a sound intruded upon her reverie.

Outside on the path someone was cursing. At first, Anna was mildly annoyed to be interrupted in her process of saying goodbye to all her best recollections. Then, as the oaths continued, a grudging admiration replaced her irritation. She knew that her voice was long gone to a whisper audible only to someone whose ear was almost touching her face, so she did not even consider trying to shout, and since all she had been able to move in more than a day were her eyelids and lips, the thought of knocking over something to attract attention was out of the question. Anna listened, because there was nothing else she could do.

The cursing was peculiarly good-natured, as if the person who spoke was aware that swearing does neither good nor harm, but does serve to relieve feelings. The voice was fluent, and it tied the words together into intricate sentences of inventive abuse, without repetition. A full, rich, rhythmic panoply of invective was visited upon a stone in a shoe, many blisters, the path that had caused it all, and the general intractability of the universe.

Anna had been listening for some time before it came to her attention that she heard the voice of a young woman.

I should have noticed it from the first, thought Anna. *I wonder who she is.*

The voice obligingly answered her mute question.

"Well, sure as my name is Jenny and that I intend to live my own life free, however short it may be, I'll take my chances on that abandoned cottage and sleep with a roof over my head, whatever happens."

There was a limping step at the door, and a few more well chosen oaths as a bare, blistered foot scuffed in larch needles. Then the last rays of sunset streamed between the peaks of the distant mountains and through the doorway, and Anna saw the silhouette of a woman holding a shoe in one hand as she reached with the other to push the door wide open.

"Whew!" said the woman who called herself Jenny. "It smells as if something had died in here."

"Not quite," said Anna, too weak for her lips to do more than frame the words. "But very close."

"Still, there's rain or snow coming," said Jenny, stepping inside. "And a roof's a roof."

Anna lay patiently on her bed. She had decided that she liked what she had heard and seen, but she had no illusions about the capacity of people to walk away from ugliness or distress. She waited to find out what would happen with hope, but without great expectation. Hands fumbled the table, and Anna offered her thoughts to guide them to a tinder box and an oil bottle that for days had been out of her reach. A spark flashed in the darkening cottage, and by its spurt of orange fire the lamp and bottle gleamed briefly. A shod and a bare foot alternately clumped and padded, oil glugged, the tinder box scraped again, and after a few moments of blowing interspersed with more oaths, the lamp flickered into light. Anna saw a bare arm downed with fine, fair hair, caught a glimpse of an upturned nose, and saw the gleam of blonde hair above the swelling curves of a robust figure.

"Table, cupboard, chair, cloak at the door, shoes," itemized Jenny. "Whoever owns this place must be... Oh Mother!"

The lamp she had held high sank in Jenny's hand, and she approached the bed slowly.

"All I need," she muttered. "A corpse to remind me of what's in my future."

Anna closed her eyes and opened them.

"Spirit of Life!" exclaimed Jenny. "She's alive!"

Anna heard the pad-clomp, pad-clomp of receding footsteps, and sighed.

Ah well, she thought. *I'd better go back to my dying as if I hadn't been interrupted.*

She closed her eyes and tried not to listen. However, moments later the bedclothes were lifted and embarrassment disrupted the equanimity she had achieved at the extremity of her life, because she knew how dirty she had become.

"First the inside, then the outside," said Jenny.

She raised Anna's head and water trickled into the old woman's mouth, and also down her cheeks and neck. The drink came long after Anna had given up all thought of the raging thirst that had consumed her a day before. A part of her mind almost rejected the gift of life-giving water, but her body took care of her needs. She felt the liquid pour down her throat, and she was once more aware of her limbs. It was not a wholly pleasurable event, but it reminded her of living, and she lived.

For the next while, Jenny nursed Anna with a solicitude and tenderness quite at variance with her continuous flow of colorful invective. The good-humored abuse was exclusively directed at the situation, never at Anna, and as each moment passed the old woman felt her affection for Jenny grow. Gradually, as first drink and then a thin gruel of porridge was spooned carefully into her mouth, Anna regained enough strength to whisper a few words of instruction as to where her belongings were kept. At last, as she lay in a freshly made bed, her body clean and nourished, the last thing Anna heard that night was Jenny grumbling to herself as she made a bed of bracken and blankets on the floor.

When morning sunlight dappled Anna's counterpane and warmed the knuckles of her gnarled hands, she heard water slosh in a pail to the tune of a ribald song she had first heard when Peder the Wizard had over-indulged in spruce beer on a midsummer's night many years before. When Jenny returned from the stream nearby, Anna relished the sight of the young woman's gleaming hair, full figure and kilted skirts above blistered feet no longer imprisoned by the shoes that had bruised them.

"Good morning, Jenny," said Anna softly.

"Oh good," said Jenny. "You're awake. Now we shall have some breakfast."

When both of them had eaten, the one a hearty bowl of nut porridge and the other a few mouthfuls, they looked at each other, evaluating.

"You're not going to die," said Jenny.

"Not yet," agreed Anna.

"Who can I fetch to help you?"

Pillowed into a half-sitting position, Anna shrugged her misshapen shoulders.

"No one. All who cared for me are long dead."

"Men," snorted Jenny.

"I recall one I remember kindly, and always will," said Anna.

"They can be fun," admitted Jenny, crossing one leg over her knee and examining her blistered toes. "I'm not one to forgo the squeezes and hugs, or the occasional midnight kisses."

"Good," said Anna. "But there's more."

"So I thought," said Jenny, her wide-spaced eyes steady. "But I don't think I believe it any more."

"So bitter, so young," said Anna.

"So bruised, so tired, so pursued by a man who insists he owns my body and soul," snapped Jenny. "And so pregnant. I hate him and his child."

"Hate him if you wish," said Anna softly. "Though it will do you no good. But not the child."

"It's his way of controlling me. It's no child of love. I should never have married him, but what can an orphan tavern wench do when she thinks she's found a way out of the pots and the bottles, the unwanted pinches and the long hours? I know better now, but he seemed a fine fellow when he courted me."

"Then remember that, and bear the child in joy."

"Not much chance. He's less than a day behind. He'll find me, and I and his child will die together. You don't know his temper. I do."

"Stop calling the child his!" said Anna curtly. "The child is its own self. You're lucky enough to bear it."

"Even a witch could do the same," rejoined Jenny.

"Not all of them," said Anna.

"Oh Mother!" exclaimed Jenny. "It's the words. They bounce out of my mouth too fast, and then I regret them. I should'a guessed. You're a witch, and your body is such that..."

"That children were impossible, even had a man looked at me as he might towards a wife," completed Anna. "And I'm no more a witch than Peder was a wizard. But he came too late. I'm ugly. That's all."

"You are not," replied Jenny. "You're beautiful. It's just that your body's a bit... a bit twisted. But I've seen no finer a face, nor no more lovely a pair of eyes than yours."

Anna stared at Jenny in momentary fear of mockery or pity, but saw only the same direct, wide-eyed stare from the woman's blue eyes.

"You have no guile, Jenny."

"Oh, I can be sneaky," said Jenny, and winked roguishly as she got up to wash the dishes.

"You can play the game of love, girl. That's different. You should not have your life poisoned."

Jenny shrugged.

"He's got to catch me first. If I can go beyond the Village without someone seeing me, they may tell him he's come the wrong way, and I'll be free of him."

At that moment, the sound of baying hounds came distantly in the mountain air. An earthenware bowl smashed to the floor as Jenny's hands flew to her face.

"No," she whispered. "Not Kurt's dogs. I don't want to die that way. He starves them to desperation and then lets them tear their prey alive. He threatened me with them when I'd not share myself with his customers in the tavern."

"Is this true, Jenny?"

Jenny turned towards the older woman, her fair hair flaring to each side of her face.

"Yes, it is," said Anna. "Very well, we must stop them and him. Build up the fire, and bring me that book on the manteltree. Open it to where it says 'Dragons.'"

"Orphans in taverns learn a lot — but not their letters," said Jenny.

"Very well, you must find the place with me," said Anna. "Be quick," she added, as the sound of the hounds came closer.

Unsure whether she was more afraid of Anna's spells than the approaching danger, Jenny nonetheless did as she was asked. She turned pages, cast herbs into the fire, poured water on the hearth, repeated strange syllables and obediently fanned the blue flames that spurted from the fire. The hounds' belling came closer and closer, the echoes clashing ever more quickly. A shouting voice joined the dogs' clamoring, and Jenny glanced at the door.

"Anna, it's not working. Thank you for trying, but it's too late. Perhaps it's because I don't believe in what I'm doing, and if so, I'm sorry. But I can't stay here and have him kill you, too. I'm going."

As she took a running step towards the door, it was slammed shut from outside by a violent gust of hot wind.

"If you leave me, I'll die anyway," said Anna. "You wretched elemental, hurry!"

The barking changed to full-throated baying as the hounds surrounded the cottage.

"Come out, Jenny!" roared a man's voice. "Or I'll set fire to the cottage. You ran from me, and now you shall suffer."

"Go knot yourself around a rope and hang your head in a shark's mouth, Kurt, you cowardly dogfish!" screamed Jenny, snatching up a carving knife.

Anna continued to mumble her spells as a rich flow of invective poured from the tavern girl.

"...and may you burn there," screamed Jenny as she finally ran out of breath.

The cottage boomed like a beaten drum, and the roof creaked under a great weight. Above was a hissing and roaring like a mighty blast furnace, and the one small window was slapped by a writhing, scaly tail.

"What would you here, man?" said an awful voice from above.

The two women looked at each other, while outside the dogs whined in fright.

"I came to take home my woman and my child that she bears," said Kurt in the tones of a man more sinned against than sinning.

"Nonsense," said the terrible voice. "You came to revenge yourself upon her."

"Not I, great Dragon," persuaded Kurt. "I came only to take what is mine and care for it with gentleness. I wish only to tenderly correct her mistakes and curb her headstrong nature and..."

"Lies!" roared the Dragon. "I, Santosh Raal-Zurmath, loathe lies. Repent of them!"

"Oh Dragon, what can I do for you?" Kurt wheedled. "I know. Why don't you have my woman? She is tender and plump and would make you a pleasant meal. Pull her out of the cottage, devour her, and let me go free."

"Cowardice!" seethed the Dragon. "I detest it still more."

The air in the cottage grew hot as an oven. The Dragon's tail struck at the walls, and wherever it touched, smoke arose.

"Don't overdo it, Santosh," said Anna crisply. "We want to be rescued, not baked alive."

The sound of running feet came to the women above the crackling from a sudden blue flare on the hearth. A flash of light flooded the small room, and a clap of thunder blew the door open. Jenny flung herself to the floor with her hands over her ears. A coiling, flaming shape streaked into the sky above the mountain peaks, and below where the path curved towards the cottage was column of oily smoke. Beside it were five smaller burning patches in the grass and mosses.

"Well," said Anna with a sniff at the sulfurous reek in the cottage, "I wish Peder had seen that. He never had much time for Santosh Raal-Zurmath, but I say that's a Dragon who knows his business!"

"Sweet Mother," gasped Jenny. "I'll never doubt you again, Anna."

"Good," said Anna. "Because I've a lot to teach you, and not much time. First you must learn to read. Then there's herb lore and woods learning, and childbirthing — we mustn't forget that — and spells and incantations and...."

She broke off and looked anxiously at Jenny.

"You will stay?" she asked very softly.

"Of course," said Jenny, as she got up from the floor and shook larch needles from her hair. "When do we start?"

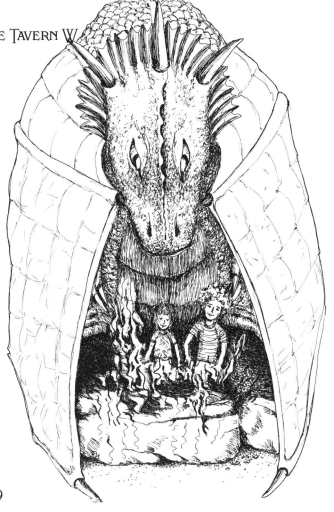

"I liked that one," said Petra. "Anna knew her own mind, and so did Jenny."

"Santosh Raal-Zurmath was a terrific Dragon, too," said Daniel. "Poof! And Kurt's up in smoke!"

"Are you a fire Dragon, too?" asked Petra.

"I have my moments," said the Dragon modestly.

"I only asked," said Petra, "because it's getting sort of cold, and I wondered, if we collected some driftwood, whether you'd mind if we built a fire."

"Watch," said the Dragon.

The huge head reared high above them and the nostrils pointed downwards at the rock on which his scaly chin had rested. There was a sound like escaping steam, and the rock started to glow. In moments, the air warmed within the tented wings the Dragon folded around the two children. Daniel held out his hands to the rock and toasted his fingers appreciatively.

"Does this mean you're going to tell us another story?" asked Petra.

"Daniel, you said that the Princess would have a good life," said the Dragon. "Would you like to hear another story about her?"

"Oh, yes," chorused Petra and Daniel.

And the Dragon told the story of The Queen and the Sea Rover.

eleven

The Queen and the Sea Rover

He was called Black Wolf by his men, and he was a sea-roving pirate who knew no law save his own will. Though his crew had acquired every vice and depravity they could discover, they were merely his instruments, welded together into a composite of their own evil by his leadership. There was something in Black Wolf that challenged decency, defiled humanity and denied compassion, but he was reasoning in his unreasonable pursuit of power: he knew it was only in the moment of subjugating another that he could experience the terrible joy of inflicting pain. He did not seek to repeat or remember these moments, only to turn from them swiftly and imagine yet another.

His inventions were beyond the scope of his men. They followed his orders, aghast at what they did, appalled that he could always find some new way to wring pleasure from the agony of others. What drove Black Wolf was not the lust for battle, rape, pillage and loot that his crew had learned long before they joined him. He was a connoisseur of other's despair. He had been known to throw a treasure into the sea in the sight of the dying man from whom he had wrenched it. He took pleasure in perverting men from their gods and principles and then flinging their own apostasy in their faces. He was capable of torturing a woman for the life of her baby, then in her last moment of hope, killing the child before her eyes and letting her go free.

Black Wolf had stolen ashore to the Village with two of his men, captured Caspar, the Queen's grandson, and taken him back to the rocky offshore island where his ship was hidden. There, under the flaring light of smoky torches, he had set about acquiring all the knowledge of the Castle that he could dredge from the boy's mind. Caspar must have known that Black Wolf was a man with no mercy or forbearance, for he took refuge in a silence so obdurate that the pirate eventually decided the boy was dumb or weak minded, and in a moment of uncharacteristic exasperation, killed him long before he had suffered all the calculating brutality of which the sea rover was capable.

Perhaps Black Wolf realized that he had made one of his rare mistakes, perhaps he wished to impress his crew with callousness, perhaps he wished to terrify the Villagers, but for whatever reason he threw Caspar's body on the rising tide and let it float ashore to be washed into the little bay at the foot of the Castle.

It chanced that Caspar's grandmother was walking the battlements above the sea when she saw the waves roll a red-coated form towards the shore and recognized the garment she herself had made. The Queen stood still, her long blue cloak sweeping the dark stone, her hands pressed together in an unspoken prayer that it was not as she feared. She sped down the granite steps, sure-footed as she had run to her boat when still a Princess, and waded into the surging water to receive Caspar's body as the waves carried him to her. She took her grandson in her arms and looked on his battered face in silence. Her long white hair fell forward about his face, enclosing her grief to his sightless eyes alone. Her silent tears fell into the salt sea and mingled in a long, wet trail from her sodden cloak behind her as she carried Caspar's body all the way up the stone stairs to her apartments.

The Queen summoned her attendants and daughter-in-law in a voice void of hope. While they cried, wailed and murmured of revenge, she stood apart with her back straight and her chin firm. In her blue eyes was a steely determination that was not to be washed away by tears alone.

Her cloak and dress still wet about her, she called for the chief men of the Castle and the Village. When her advisors expressed their outrage, sympathy and condolences, she abruptly focused their attention on the meaning of this hideous act, and demanded that they immediately make preparations for the defense of the Castle. At last, having shared out responsibilities to the men and women most likely to keep their nerve, she abruptly dismissed them and strode from the council hall before they could leave. The years as princess, queen, mother of a king and regent after his untimely death lent her voice an authority that sent them hastening to obey her commands. Yet she knew larger villages and stronger castles had fallen prey to sea rovers, and she had heard from her followers the counsels of despair.

The Queen swept past the women of the Castle who would have detained her with dry clothes and sympathetic talk, and sought out her granddaughter. The little girl had been forgotten in the woe of mourning and bustle of preparations, and had only the company of her favorite doll to console her.

"Come, Kirsten," said the Queen. "Dry your tears. We have women's work."

She took the little girl's hand in hers and together they walked the stone corridors of the Castle, Kirsten hurrying to keep up with her grandmother's smooth strides. Past guards readying weapons, men and women hurrying to prepare for siege and the astonished stares of counselors who tried to stay her, the Queen led her granddaughter through her apartments and back down the long stone stair leading to the breakwater behind which was moored her little boat, the *Spindrift*. Together they loosed the braided ropes. The Queen lifted Kirsten into the stern and gave her charge of the tiller while she readied the sails.

Disregarding the cries of her daughter-in-law and the protests of the councilors who hurried to the breakwater, their court robes splashed by spray, the Queen and the little Princess sailed out of the protected bay into the fjord. Kirsten's eyes were wide with excitement and apprehension, but she steered the *Spindrift* skillfully and never questioned her grandmother's will.

When they were flying seaward in a rising wind, the sails straining and the slim boat's bow rising spray-wreathed above the waves, the Queen took off her cloak and wrapped it around Kirsten. Her dress wind-blown, and her white hair tangling behind her, she stood beside the mast and scanned the horizon towards which they sailed. The little Princess shivered, then she, too, stiffened her back, raised her chin and devoted herself to keeping the *Spindrift*'s course straight and true as she responded to every vagary of wind and water.

When the Village and Castle were no longer visible and the looming mountains alone marked where they had begun their quest, the Queen nodded once and pointed towards blue-black dolphins bursting from the smooth curves of the waves. The *Spindrift* chased down the wind towards the creatures of the sea, and Kirsten was joined by her grandmother at the tiller. As she had done when still a girl, the Queen knotted a rope about her, taking only her sailor's knife in one hand, and poised herself on the heaving boat.

"Kirsten," she said, "I am no longer supple and firm-fleshed as I once was, but I must nonetheless reach the emissaries of the great Sea Mother. Be sure you keep the *Spindrift* on course, and whatever may befall, do not be afraid."

So saying, the Queen plunged into the sea to join the dolphins romping around the little boat. As the water closed over her, she felt how much her strength had lessened with the years, but that knowledge did not alter her unswerving purpose. Arms outstretched to the dolphins, she dived down with them until her aching lungs demanded she return to the surface, and then still further. With one quick slash of her knife, she severed the rope that held her, but made no vain struggle to regain the world of air. The ever-smiling faces of the dolphins came close, and their bottle-smooth heads nuzzled her body. Then the eldest swam deep in the dark waters and presented her broad back to carry the Queen upward. The lesser dolphins in attendance, they surged upward faster than the rising column of bubbles which, despite every effort, her lips could not restrain. When they reached the rising and falling waves, the dolphins buoyed up the spent human body as one of their own.

So it was that the Queen did not see the sleek, plunging messenger when it left the clustered sea creatures, nor did she feel the sea rise around her as if a mountain had pushed up from the ocean floor. When she opened her eyes, she sighed in the extremity of her exhaustion and thankfulness, for the Queen recognized the huge hand in which she was held and knew the presence of Ke-Au-Ka Ida. At length, when she felt her strength return, she tried to rise.

"Lie still, my child," said the gentle voice of Ke-Au-Ka Ida. "You are over-spent, and I need no reverence from one who has so bravely lived as you."

"I did not come to beseech you for my husband's life when it was taken from him, nor would I trouble you with my grief now that his son is no more," said the Queen.

"I know it," said the great Sea Dragon. "And I know as well the reason that you have sought me out, but not what you would ask of me."

"I would that my grandchild live to see the Village spared," said the Queen. "For myself I ask nothing save that my life may be a small recompense for my wish."

"Ah, Princess that was and Queen that is, you would bargain with an elemental, but you know not the cost. You are willing to forfeit your life, but you must offer still more."

"Speak, Great Mother."

And Ke-Au-Ka Ida, knowing the bargain sealed, sent a vision to the Queen. She saw her Castle blazing in the darkness of a winter's night, then gnawed into a ruin by years without number. Strange ships with no sails coursed below the seas while wars were fought by desperate men bringing death to young and old alike.

The Queen watched her dream of the future unfold, and shuddered. At last she saw children play on the broken stair down which she had run as child and woman, Princess and Queen. Covering her face, she rose to her knees, her feet, and finally stood on the great Dragon's hand below that huge head that looked down on her as it had once before. She echoed as best she could the deep obeisance she had made so long ago, and though her body was no longer supple with youth, she was nonetheless graceful as ever, and her spirit was no less determined.

"I thank you, Ke-Au-Ka Ida, that you did not show me my granddaughter's death. I would not have you stay all the chances and changes of time. Only guard her from this present danger."

The great eye of Ke-Au-Ka Ida looked deep into the Queen's soul, and the Dragon was pleased by what she saw.

"Your heart holds only justice, love and mercy. Revenge did not bring you to me. Were it otherwise…"

When the Dragon left her thoughts unsaid, the Queen spoke quietly.

"I know that all must pass away, Great Mother, and I am as prepared as any mortal can be."

The mighty gaze of the Elemental was fixed upon her, and Ke-Au-Ka Ida's mind felt the Queen's inmost pang of knowing that she must leave the world in which she craved to linger.

"My child," said the great Sea Mother, "Since you have offered me your longing for life and held nothing back, you will be answered."

Hope had left the watchers on the Castle walls. They spoke of the madness of despair in which their Queen had left them, and looked seaward toward their doom. Sailing toward them was a black-sailed ship wherein armed men shouted threats of destruction. Then, as the Villagers trembled and the guards made fearful readiness for defense, a sudden sea mist arose, twisting winds wrestled together and spray tumbled upon itself in fountains reaching to the clouds. A white wall of churning water raced up the fjord toward the doomed ship, and as it closed around the vessel a scream of defiance came from Black Wolf. Roiling water fell hissing into the sea, and the eerie storm was gone as fast as it had arisen.

Sailing amid the wreckage of what had been the raiders' ship came the *Spindrift*, her sails filled by a favorable wind. With cries of amazement the Villagers ran to the water's edge and surrounded the little bay as through the narrow passage at the breakwater came the slim boat, steered by the little Princess. And as they watched and cheered, they saw their Queen standing in her long blue cloak, one hand upon her granddaughter's shoulder. They could not see Kirsten's shining eyes, nor hear what she whispered to the Queen.

"Grandmother," said the little Princess. "Ke-Au-Ka Ida spoke to me, and called me her child."

"And so she did to me," replied the Queen.

Their hands touched and held upon the tiller. Princess and Queen guided the *Spindrift* to her moorings below the Castle walls.

"That was here," said Daniel, looking through the archway of the Dragon's wings at the little bay. "When the Castle was still her home."

"Poor Queen," said Petra. "To see her lovely Castle all ruined."

"But she won," said Daniel. "Except, it wasn't like a battle, was it? She didn't seem to even hate Black Wolf."

"I think I would, if it had been my grandson," said Petra slowly. "She was special. I wish I'd been her grand-daughter."

"I'll ignore that," said the Dragon.

"It was all so long ago," said Daniel. "Are we the only people to have met a Dragon since then?"

121

The Dragon shook its massive head.

"It's not often that folk today get to meet us," it said. "But it happens. Listen to me for the last time."

And the Dragon told the story of Dragon Dawn.

twelve

Dragon Dawn

There were two young people who had lived in the Village beside the fjord for all of their lives. They had played together as children, shared adventures in the high alpine valleys and on the cold, clear waters of the fjord, and had come to trust each other far beyond the habit of regular meetings. They had spoken openly of those private moments with other people that need to be told only to true friends, and they still were secure in their friendship even though they knew a great deal about each other, not all of it pleasant to remember.

Because of this bond that went beyond liking David turned to Marion when he found himself aware that he could no longer live in the Village. His decision was more the result of feelings than thoughts. When he spoke to her, it was of a desire to see more of the world than was visible beneath the shouldering mountains, and of a dissatisfaction with a life he found increasingly constrained and repetitive. But behind his words was something to which he could not put a name.

Marion listened to the hopes and plans that burst disjointedly from David as they sat together at sunset below the ruined Castle, and as he spoke she felt a deep understanding that went beyond what his words said. He punctuated his outbursts by kicking at the gravelly beach or prodding at the sand with a stick, while she sat with her chin in both her hands, looking into the dwindling light through wisps of hair fluttered across her face by the evening wind.

"It's like the Castle," said David, after a long silence broken only by the hush of the rising tide. "Once there was greatness here. The Queen who defeated Black Wolf, the wizards of the foothills, the harpers and the warriors — they knew they were alive. Sometimes I look around me and wonder if the folk in the Village think of anything beyond their next meal."

Marion nodded. She was a person whose silences were eloquent with understanding.

"The old ones," continued David, "sometimes have the look of people who have seen mystery, but now they don't believe in anything they can't hold in their hands. They've lost wonder, and their best memories they call fantasies and myths."

Marion put a hand on David's arm, and he looked at her long, slim fingers. It struck him that of everything to which he was about to say farewell, Marion's hands would be the most difficult.

"Come with me tomorrow," he said, suddenly standing up from the rock on which he had been sitting. "We'll take my boat out to Black Wolf's lair and watch the sun rise."

Marion nodded. They walked together back to the Village, and when they said goodnight at her door, they discovered that they had been hand in hand since leaving the beach.

Before the sun rose on the next day, David was in his boat, *The Laughing Princess*. Sure-handed in the darkness, he made sail and singled up his lines to the quay. Then he sat in the sternsheets, gnawing at his thumbnail, wondering whether Marion would appear. When he no longer knew if he would go alone, go back home to bed, or go slightly mad and sail out into the ocean without food or water, he heard a soft footfall above him on the quay below which his boat rose and fell to the waves.

"David?" she softly asked the darkness.

"Marion," he replied in a whisper.

She passed down a basket she had secretly filled with food from her mother's larder, and climbed down from the stone wharf into the little boat.

"Let's go," whispered David. "Take the jib-sheet, and we'll be off on the starboard tack."

"Got it," replied Marion.

"Why are we whispering?" asked David.

"It felt right," said Marion. "I've been tip-toeing around the house, hushing the dogs and telling them that they couldn't come with me, and now I don't want to stop."

"Cast off!" said David.

A rope splashed into the sea as he obeyed his own order. He hauled the mainsail to the masthead, then when the before-dawn wind caught the canvass, *The Laughing Princess* seemed to come alive. The ripples drumming under the boat's bow, they rushed towards a horizon where the last and brightest constellation sank into the ocean.

Though they both had known the fjord all their lives, they were nonetheless alert beyond usual awareness as they sped through the darkness. Guided by starshine and their memories of where rocks jutted out from the cliffs, they sailed *The Laughing Princess* as if one mind controlled their two bodies, and yet they were acutely conscious of how separate and alone they both were.

Once the few lights left burning nightlong in the Village were far behind them, and the mountains were a ragged blackness where there were no stars, they altered course for the island where tradition held it that Black Wolf had hidden before his attack on the Village.

"Do you suppose there ever was a Black Wolf?" asked Marion, and then chuckled. "Silly question to ask a man who calls his boat *The Laughing Princess.*"

"I have a little difficulty imagining the Dragon," confessed David. "But then, so did all the artists who tried to draw it on shields and in the picture books we looked at when we were young."

Their voices came to each other out of the night as if disembodied, even though they sat close enough to have touched.

"David," said Marion, after a long silence. "I'm leaving the Village as well."

David's hand on the tiller moved of its own accord, and the sail flapped once before he brought *The Laughing Princess* back onto course.

"I didn't know it until now," he said to the night, "but I wanted you to be here when... if I return."

"After you first told me you were leaving, I wanted to be here waiting for you," said Marion. "But..."

"Nobody else would have understood," interrupted David.

"Yes," said Marion. "But the reasons why you told me are also part of why I must leave as well, and you're the only one who can understand that."

"But we..." began David.

"...may never meet again?" asked Marion.

"I have a great deal of difficulty imagining that," said David slowly.

"More than with the Dragon?" asked Marion.

"About the same," replied David.

They sailed in silence while brightness grew behind the mountains, and every moment there were fewer and fewer stars. The sails they tended ghosted grey as in the east the sky turned first green, then yellow. Suddenly, molten gold spilled upwards above them as the sun rose over the mountains. Rose-pink light warmed first their boat and a heartbeat later the tops of the cresting waves. David and Marion looked at each other as if they had never met, both of them seeing every detail of a face they had known so well as to have almost forgotten.

The sun turned into an orange mist behind a white band of cloud that rushed across the horizon, and the mountaintops glowed white-gold, their snowcaps luminous.

"Magic," said Marion, as she pointed to the east.

David nodded.

"Dragon dawn," he said. "The sort of morning when... What's that?"

Ahead of them, the ocean was in turmoil, waves seething together from every direction. David altered course, but as soon as he did, another patch of sea turned into a fountain of spray. When he steered between the two threats, a fog bank rolled towards *The Laughing Princess*. He looked over his shoulder, preparing to turn towards the shore, and caught sight of what Marion stared at in amazement. Out of the sunrise flew shapes that were not birds. From the mountains appeared forms hard-edged as the rocks over which they soared. Glowing in the dawn light, spiraling and turning in the air, their jeweled bodies gleaming, Dragons were assembling above the very place where their boat sailed.

"This isn't happening," said David. "Tell me this isn't happening, Marion."

"Hush," said Marion. "They're talking."

David clutched the tiller of his boat as the mainsheet went slack in his other hand. Becalmed under a circle of flying shapes out of another time, they stared upward past the slack sails into a weave of interlocked spirals made by the winged creatures above them. The web of flying Dragons whirled in a shimmering circle around *The Laughing Princess*. David and Marion were inside a column made entirely of soaring and diving Dragons, now descending to where the sea wetted their scales until they shone, now rising into the clouds of spray their fiery breath had turned to coiling steam.

"Change," whispered Marion in a strange voice. "Change we must, and change we shall. An age is past since last we met. Another age, and we hope to meet, in another age we may return. Change we must, and change we shall, but change shall be at our own choice, and in that change we shall rejoice."

Then David heard the voices as well: mist-soft, sleet-harsh, diamond-clear, thunder-deep. And the coil of Dragons tightened around them until their boat was spun around and around on an eddying twirl of water and air that grew into a foaming funnel. David sawed the tiller back and forth, trying vainly to fill the flapping sails with gusts of wind which came from every direction.

"Marion!" he shouted. "Hold on!"

The Laughing Princess was sucked down into the maelstrom. Deeper and deeper they slid towards a sinister bubble of foam at the vortex, and then, as David reached towards Marion with one hand to grapple her to him and cling to the boat which was their only chance of staying alive, the sea smoothed and they rose back to the surface. Above them the sky was clear, and the sun slanted across an ocean empty save for a head-high dome of white, half sunk below the waves a mere arm's length away. As they watched, the mound of glittering bubbles fell hissing into the sea, and beside them bobbed a small, oval shape no bigger than Marion's fist. She leaned over the side of the boat and scooped it up in her palm, where it glowed in the morning light with an iridescent sheen. She cupped her long fingers around the mother-of-pearl egg, and they bent their heads together in wonder.

"Put it back," said David slowly, as if someone else had charge of his voice.

"...into the sea from where it came," continued Marion, as she lowered the egg tenderly into the water.

They stared at each other, confounded by the sense of having spoken words they had not intended. The sails of *The Laughing Princess* filled, and the little boat drew away from where the sunlight glowed on the bobbing egg. As they watched, its gleaming shell was raised up and held above the waves, encircled in a huge hand. There was a swirl of troubled water, and the sea trembled in its depths.

It was some time before David and Marion realized that they were sitting close together, sailing on their original course as if nothing had happened.

"I'm taking passage on this week's trading ship," said Marion calmly.

"I leave tomorrow on a south-bound fishing boat," said David.

"We have today..." began Marion.

"...and the food you brought, and the island to explore, and..."

David paused.

"...and sailing with *The Laughing Princess,*" said Marion. "David, now do you believe she really met a Dragon?"

Their hands met and held very tightly. Then, as the sails caught a puff of wind and spray flew into their faces, their fingers parted and they laughed together, even though in their mouths was the taste of salt.

Daniel and Petra huddled close around the warm rock, and over their shoulders heard the thudding of a small boat's engine. They turned and saw their parents waving in the bow of a fishing boat that was passing the ruined breakwater and entering the little bay. The two children ran to meet the boat as its bow crunched gently into the shore.

"Climb in," said their father. "We have news for you."

"What have you been doing all day?" asked their mother.

"Oh, exploring," said Daniel.

Petra stared at the empty beach with her mouth open, and said nothing.

"What have you got in your hands?" asked their father.

Daniel and Petra both looked and saw the translucent, gleaming eggshell halves which they were holding. Without so much as a glance at each other, they slid their gifts into their pockets, and clambered into the fishing boat.

"Would you be very disappointed if we didn't go any further?" asked their mother. "We've just seen a little cottage we can rent for the rest of our holiday. The people who own it travel a lot."

"It's beside the sea," said their father, "and there's a little sailboat that comes with it."

"I could learn to sail?" asked Daniel.

"Me too!" said Petra.

Their parents nodded.

"You'll like the boat," said their father. "It has an unusual name from a local legend. It's all mythological stuff, full of Dragons and pirates and..."

"*The Laughing Princess!*" said Petra and Daniel at the same moment.

The fishing boat's engine rumbled, making further conversation impossible. Water swirled around the propeller, and they chugged into the fjord past the breakwater below the ruined Castle.

Petra suddenly grabbed Daniel's arm and pointed. High above the granite blocks at the top of the tower, glowing in the evening light of the setting sun, a winged creature spiraled gleaming into the sky.

About the Author and the Illustrator

Seymour Hamilton lives in Chelsea, Quebec, Canada. He spent half his working life teaching English Literature, and the other as a writer/editor. Since retiring, he has been reviving his unpublished stories and making them available as podcasts.

You can find out more by going to SeymourHamilton.com. There, you'll discover how the book came to be written, as well as links to free podcasts of The *Astreya* Trilogy and *The Laughing Princess,* read by the author.

Canadian artist and illustrator Shirley MacKenzie likes to travel. Sometimes her destinations take her to places that are fashioned to teach, like a turn-of-the-century tool museum in Lanark County, Ontario. She meandered through historical sketches of an Acadian Village in Nova Scotia, toured elementary students through halls of Canadian art, operated a nineteenth-century grist mill, and showcased the hidden gems of Europe and Great Britain with her paintings. More recently, Shirley's book illustration has expanded her map. Here she has found more fantastic places to discover and illuminate. Find out more at www.artspace59.com.

Did you enjoy this book? If so, please share your thoughts with other readers on Amazon.com, BN.com, Goodreads.com or your favorite book site. The author is happy to hear from you via his Goodreads page or his website, SeymourHamilton.com.

≈❧

ALSO BY SEYMOUR HAMILTON

Novels

The *Astreya* Trilogy:

Astreya I: The Voyage South • *Astreya II: The Men of the Sea* • *Astreya III: The Wanderer's Curse*

Stories

The Laughing Princess
(Listen to it at Podiobooks.com)
(also in Spanish as *La Princesa valiente*)